"I've found m
Catherine mu

"Who," Luke asked dangerously, "is he?"

"I'd rather not say right now. But before I do anything, I'd like you to give me some pointers." She gave him a guileless look. "Your input will be invaluable, because…because he's very much like you."

"Like me?"

"You know. Sexy. Sophisticated. A ladies' man."

Luke groaned. "A player." He raked his fingers through his hair until it stood up like a cock's comb.

Catherine smiled. "Exactly. If anyone can tell me how to seduce a player, you'd be the one."

Luke leaned closer, crowding her. "You want *me* to teach you how to seduce a man?"

"Don't think you can?" Cat taunted.

"If I wanted to, which I don't, I could."

Cat grinned. "Bet you can't."

Dear Reader,

The month of June is hot, hot, hot. It's time
for skimpy clothing, barbecues, shady trees and
swimming. Anything to keep cool. Cat and Luke's
story isn't going to help you achieve that goal.

Catherine Harris has quietly adored Luke Van Buren
since she was a child. But Luke's a man with scruples
and honor to spare. He made her a promise then, a
promise he stubbornly refuses to break *now*. Catherine
is determined to change his mind. By the time she's
finished with him, poor Luke will not only have
forgotten that long-ago vow, he'll have forgotten his
own name.

Ah, the power of love.

I hope you enjoy Catherine's seduction of Mr. Right.
I'd love to hear from you. Please write to me at
P.O. Box 1686, Kent, WA 98035, or visit my
Web site at www.cherryadair.com, or e-mail me
at cherryadair@qwest.net.

Happy reading,

Cherry Adair

Books by Cherry Adair

HARLEQUIN TEMPTATION
492—THE MERCENARY

SEDUCING MR. RIGHT
Cherry Adair

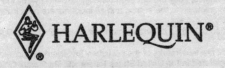

HARLEQUIN®

TORONTO • NEW YORK • LONDON
AMSTERDAM • PARIS • SYDNEY • HAMBURG
STOCKHOLM • ATHENS • TOKYO • MILAN • MADRID
PRAGUE • WARSAW • BUDAPEST • AUCKLAND

For Jean Reed, friend and mentor, with love.
Gone, but never forgotten.
This one was always for you.

ISBN 0-373-25933-6

SEDUCING MR. RIGHT

Copyright © 2001 by Cherry Wilkinson.

This edition published by arrangement with Harlequin Books S.A.

® and TM are trademarks of the publisher. Trademarks indicated with
® are registered in the United States Patent and Trademark Office, the
Canadian Trade Marks Office and in other countries.

Visit us at www.eHarlequin.com

Printed in U.S.A.

1

THREE THINGS OCCURRED to Catherine Harris as she jerked out of a dead sleep.

One, she was stark naked in Luke Van Buren's bed.

Two, he was about to enter his bedroom.

Three, he wasn't alone. A woman's throaty laughter mingled with Luke's deep baritone in the hallway.

Luke wasn't supposed to be back in San Francisco for a couple more days. Catherine tried not to panic. Suddenly years of planning didn't seem like nearly enough time.

She leaned up on one elbow, squinted into the darkness and remembered she'd thrown her bra over the clock to block the red LCD light. Catherine flopped back on the pillow, several options, none of them viable, flashed through her sleep-fogged brain. Hiding under the bed while bedsprings bounced was too hideous to contemplate. As was the picture of the fire department rescuing her from the ledge outside Luke's bedroom window, twenty-two stories above the street.

She heard a soft thud. A shoe? The sound of her own rapid pulse did nothing to block out the next thump. The swish of clothing. An impatient sigh. A hungry kiss pressed to bare flesh. Framed in the open doorway, barely discernable, was Luke's white shirt, which the woman's hands were rapidly removing. Catherine saw it flutter to the carpet. Heard a click.

Oh, God. His belt buckle?

"Speak up, Catherine," she whispered.

There was the distinct rasp of a zipper.

The sound of a juicy kiss.

"Oh, Luke!" The woman giggled. Then there was more rustling, more heated murmurs, breathy sighs. Catherine's cheeks flamed, blood pounding in her ears. Anticipating the fireworks to come, she felt hysterical laughter bubbling up in her throat.

"Make love to me, Luke. Oh, yes…I adore when you touch me…yes. Mmm, Oh, yes."

Oh, no. Catherine tried to slither out of the way before the woman flopped onto the bed. Too late.

The weight of two full-grown adults squashed the air out of Catherine's lungs. Grunting, she tried to wriggle out from under, but couldn't get any traction on the satin sheets.

The woman rolled to the side, shot to her feet and let out a bloodcurdling scream. With a thump and a curse, Luke landed on the floor beside the bed.

"What in God's name—"

"There's someone in your bed!" the woman shrieked.

Catherine heard Luke get to his feet, then fumble for the switch on the bedside lamp.

Showtime.

She sat up, tucked the slithery sheet under her armpits and tried her best to appear nonchalant. Chances were she looked like the wild woman of Borneo. She hadn't braided her hair before she'd gone to bed; it frothed about her bare shoulders, tickling the tops of her breasts. The bedside light snapped on just as she blew a particularly stubborn hank out of her eyes. As she squinted in the brightness, her gaze clashed with a pair of narrowed gray-green eyes boring a hole into the middle of her forehead.

"Catherine." Luke zipped his pants, then raked his fingers through his disheveled dark hair. His broad, hairy chest expanded with the ragged, frustrated breath he dragged into his lungs.

Reluctantly she tore her gaze from his splendidly naked chest and waited for the dragon to roar. He appeared twice as tall as six foot three, and three times as irritated as he'd been when she'd backed his new sports car into the mailbox years ago.

"I might have known." He plucked her bra off the clock. "Yours?" The black sports bra hung like a limp piece of licorice in his large, well-shaped hand.

Catherine leaned forward just enough to take the bra without losing her grip on the safely tucked sheet. "Thanks." The brush of his fingers sent an electrical charge up her arm. She cleared her throat, then decided to live dangerously and fluttered her eyelashes at him. "Does this mean I have to get dressed now, honey?"

Catherine gave his friend a wide smile, which the woman didn't reciprocate. Drop-dead gorgeous in a little black number hardly wider than a belt, she had long legs and an ample bosom, displayed to advantage in the skimpy dress. Expensive, high-maintenance, honey-colored hair cascaded seductively over one shoulder. Catherine sighed. Another pocket Venus. Without a sense of humor. Figured.

Into the tension-laced atmosphere, Catherine asked brightly, "Is it your birthday?"

"What is she talking about?" the blonde demanded, hand splayed across her chest to hold up her dress. Keeping her eyes firmly fixed on Catherine, she turned her back so Luke could zip her. The twin lines between her plucked-to-a-fare-thee-well eyebrows would become permanent in short order if she persisted in scowling like that. The woman had the kind of looks that would go rapidly downhill the moment gravity took over, and a slight overbite that made her, in Catherine's opinion, look a little like a hamster she'd once owned. She also had the same mean-eyed look Scamper used to give just before he gnawed her finger.

Narrow-eyed, Luke scrutinized her. "What are you up to?"

Catherine opened her eyes so wide her lashes tickled her eyebrows. "Didn't you bring her home to play, Luke, sweetums?"

"Catherine..." he warned.

She gave him an apologetic little smile, filled with as much sincerity as she could muster, and spoke normally. "I thought you were out of town. Honestly, I wouldn't have—"

"Who the hell is she?" the woman demanded, slipping her dainty feet back into high-heeled mules, her mouth unattractively pouty.

Luke strode to the highboy against the far wall, then glanced over his shoulder. "Cat Harris. Elizabeth Wyrech." He jerked open a drawer, yanked out a sage-green cotton sweater and pulled it over his head. It did wonderful things to his eyes.

"Hi." Catherine didn't offer her hand, for the sheet was in danger of slithering into her lap. "Look, you don't have to run off. Does she, Luke? I mean—"

"Cut it out, Catherine," Luke said, clearly not amused. "Explain to Elizabeth who you are, then shut up."

Catherine stared at him. "Everything? Are you sure? Doesn't she know you get bored with just one lady in your be—"

"A ménage à trois? This is really sick, Luke." Elizabeth scooped up her purse and held it in front of her like a shield. "I'm calling a cab."

"She's my sister, for God's sake!"

"Oh, really?" No matter how beautiful, the woman had a nasty mind and an ugly sneer. Catherine narrowed her eyes at her. Elizabeth narrowed hers back.

"You have different last names."

"Different mothers," Luke said.

"Different fathers," Catherine said at the same time.

"She's my stepsister!" Luke strode across the room and wrapped his strong fingers around Catherine's clenched jaw. "Siblings. Right, Cat?" His hand moved her head up and down to acknowledge the statement.

"Right." Catherine gave Elizabeth the Wretch a tight smile and pretended that arrow hadn't pierced her heart. "His sister."

"That's even sicker," Elizabeth said coldly before storming out of the bedroom.

Catherine gripped the sheet tighter, a hard knot in her throat. She couldn't drag her eyes away from Luke, and her face flamed hotly enough for her to damn her pale skin. His sister.

From six years old she'd dreamed, wished, prayed he'd accept her as family. When she'd been older that wish had come true. But by then sister was no longer the relationship she craved.

Usually pragmatic and sensible, Catherine had made a gigantic leap of faith in coming to Luke. This was not an auspicious start to her plan.

"I'll take Liz home and be back in twenty minutes."

"I'll be here." If she didn't take a cowardly leap from the balcony first.

He turned when he got to the door and glanced back. "Don't go to sleep. We're going to talk. Tonight."

Did they have to? She checked his eyes. Absolutely.

"Be dressed when I get back."

"Aye, aye, Captain." Catherine saluted. The satin sheet glided like water over her naked skin, baring one breast.

She froze and stared at Luke.

White-knuckled, he gripped the doorknob.

A beat later he slammed the bedroom door behind him.

I'M IN DEEP, DEEP TROUBLE here, Luke thought on his circuitous, I-need-more-time-to-think-about-this drive home an hour later. How in heaven's name was he ever going to be able to forget the sight of Cat's bare b— His fingers tightened on the steering wheel. Oh, man…

His dad had married Cat's mother nineteen years ago. So there wasn't a drop of familial blood between them. Thank God. But Luke could never forget what a mean, nasty jerk he'd been to Catherine for years. It had taken even more years before he'd been forced to realize just what his cruelty was costing her, and he'd sworn to himself he would always love and protect her to make up for the years he'd done just the opposite.

The way he now felt didn't negate the promises he'd made.

He'd sworn to his dad, just before he'd died, that he would take care of Catherine. More important, he'd made Cat a promise to be her big brother. He'd assured her he would always be there for her. To protect her, to keep her safe, to have him to depend on, for anything and everything. Luke considered these promises sacrosanct, unshakable and nonnegotiable.

Too bad his libido wasn't as ethical as his brain. He reluctantly turned his decrepit Jaguar into the basement parking lot beneath his building. Just because his feelings had changed dramatically was no reason to disillusion her. He had to remember that to Cat he was no more than her big brother. Her safe, dependable big brother. End of story.

HER FACE STILL HOT, Catherine speedily dressed the second the front door closed behind Luke and what's-her-name. Her goal had seemed so simple and straightforward back home in Beaverton. Get Luke to see her as a desirable woman and act on it. Of course, she hadn't planned on him seeing her naked in his bed. At least not yet!

Catherine padded into the living room and flung herself into the squishy black leather chair she'd bought Luke with every penny of her savings when he and their friend Nick had gone off to New York to become architects. The chair smelled like Luke. She snuggled her cheek against the skin-smooth leather and closed her eyes. She'd thought of little else but him for years. She could do this. She *would* do this.

Perhaps it wasn't so bad, after all, that Luke had had a sneak preview....

WEARING JEANS and one of his old Pratt Institute sweatshirts, Cat's five-foot-ten frame was curled up in the big black leather armchair in the corner of the living room when Luke returned.

Thank God she's dressed, he thought, *and thank God she's tamed that hair.* Catherine Anne Harris had the reddest, wildest, most touchable hair he'd ever seen. It had a life of its own.

Seeing her naked in his bed with that electrified mane, like living flame gone berserk, had almost given him a coronary. He wasn't quite so tempted to bury his hands in it when she had it scraped back in her usual French braid. And if he concentrated very hard for the next three or four hundred years, he might forget how the light had sculpted, in shadows and highlights, the satin sheets on Cat's naked body. And the sight of one plump, perfect, pale freckled breast. He stuffed his hands into his pockets and sauntered into the living room.

"Hi." Cat sat up and rubbed sleepy hazel eyes, her cheeks flushed under a generous sprinkling of cinnamon-colored freckles. She pulled her bare feet up and wrapped her arms around her knees. Even her slender toes had cinnamon dots.

There was a short, strained silence. "She seems like a nice woman," Cat commented, offering a hopeful smile. Luke was caught by the humor in her eyes and the lushness of her wide, soft mouth.

He shook his head. "Not particularly." He sat on the edge of the coffee table facing her. Thank God she had no inkling how much it cost him to sit this close and not jump her bones.

Cat frowned. "I don't get it. If you don't like her, what were you doing sleeping with her?"

"A, I hadn't slept with her. Yet. B, I like Elizabeth just fine. C, don't change the subject. Not that you aren't welcome, Catwoman, but what are you doing here?" he asked mildly.

"I thought you'd gone to New York this week." She rested her chin on her bent knees. "What did you tell her?"

"I told her you have a warped sense of the ridiculous, but that basically you're harmless." About as harmless as dropping a centerfold into a maximum-security prison block.

"I was embarrassed. It was awkward for all of us. I guess I made it worse by trying to joke about it. I'm sorry to have put you in an uncomfortable position, Luke. Really. If you want me to call her—"

"There's no need, Cat. Don't worry about it." Elizabeth had the sensitivity of a newt. Anyone else would have seen Catherine's embarrassment. "I came home from New York early."

She wasn't wearing a bra. He could see her full

breasts move gently as she shifted. He frowned. "Don't distract me, answer the question. What are you doing here?"

Cat yawned, then rubbed the tip of her nose with her palm. "I was in a rut in Oregon. I needed a change, so here I am."

"You aren't going to stop day trading are you?" Luke asked, horrified. Self-taught, Cat had become a market wizard. She enjoyed the challenge of figuring out which stocks were about to go up, and buying and selling them on the same day to immediately profit on the stock's rise in value. This enabled Cat to multiply her money many times over the course of a day. Plus she'd been able to do it from home, on her own computer, while she took care of his dad. With her canny knowledge of the stock market, and uncanny intuition, she'd made a bundle of money trading stocks for Luke over the years. If it wasn't for her, he and Nick would never have been able to afford to open their own architectural business so soon. The business was doing well enough to afford them the luxury of owning their own building.

The woman had a mind like a steel trap and the Midas touch. There were several of his dad's old cronies whose money she'd parlayed into small fortunes, just for the fun of it.

"Don't worry. I brought my computer. Your future fortune is still safe in my hands."

"Thank God. You can set up camp at Van Buren and Stratton if you like. There's a spare office on the second floor you can use." The thought of being with Catherine Harris 24/7 terrified him. He wondered where he could find large amounts of saltpeter.

"You don't have to sound so unenthusiastic," Cat laughed. "No, thank you, it would never work. We all know each other too well. You're too much of a slob, and Nick and I would goof around and I'd never get any work done. If you don't mind, I'll work from here for a while."

"Sure." Cat would be here every night when he got home. A curse and a blessing.

"Did I mess up a beautiful relationship?" she asked suddenly.

Luke easily followed the non sequitur. Cat was nothing if not tenacious. "Probably not."

"Will you see her again?"

"More than likely."

"She could have given the situation the benefit of the doubt, you know." Cat nibbled her bottom lip. He wished to hell she wouldn't do that. "A little sense of humor would have gone a long way." She sighed gustily. "Okay, it was stupid, and I'm really, really sorry."

Ah, Cat's innate sense of honor and fair play. "No harm done. Don't worry about it."

"Do you mind if I stay here until I find a place of my own?"

Don't offer, he thought. *Do not, the hell, offer.* "No, not at all. I wouldn't have given you a key if I minded your comings and goings." He paused, then scowled, alarmed that his eyes kept dropping to her chest. "I told you when I came home for the funeral that you'd be welcome anytime. Why didn't you tell me you weren't happy there?"

Cat sighed. "Luke. How old am I?"

"You're...twenty-three?"

"Try twenty-six, I've always been seven years younger than you. How come you never remember?" She shifted back in his chair, clearly uncomfortable under his close scrutiny. She'd always been a prickly little thing. "Life was passing me by. I want to stretch my wings a bit."

"I know, honey." He reached out and covered her hand. Cat had nursed his father for the five years preceding his death eight months ago. Luke had frequently envied Cat and his father's close relationship. Now Luke was all Cat had left. Her flaky mother didn't count.

She flushed and withdrew her hand. "I didn't sacrifice anything. We were father and daughter by choice, not chance, and I loved him. Don't go all big brother on me. It took longer than I thought to get his affairs tied up. I contacted a real estate agent and put the house on the market—" She put up a hand to forestall his usual rhetoric about the estate. "No, Luke, I'm not keeping the house. Besides, my moth—Faith is between husbands at the moment, and she's been broadly hinting she might like to come 'home to rest' for a little while."

"She's run out of money." It wasn't a question. If Faith was between husbands or lovers, it was a given.

Cat's smile broke his heart. "That, too."

He'd like to wring Faith's beautiful neck. "You should buy a nice condo with the money Dad left you."

Those expressive tiger eyes of hers darkened. Ah, hell.

"It's invested. If you don't want me here," she said

stiffly, slender shoulders hunched, "just say so. I'll go and stay with Nick."

Nick. Their mutual friend, partner, fellow architect and ladies' man? No way. "Does Nick know about this?"

"Not yet."

At least she'd come to Luke first.

He and Nick had been next-door neighbors, and best friends, when Luke still had a matched set of parents. After the divorce, and his father's remarriage, Nick and Cat had become friends. Luke wasn't jealous of their close relationship anymore, but he was inordinately pleased she'd chosen to come to him instead of going to Nick.

"Hey! *Mi casa es su casa.* Finding an apartment in San Francisco is almost impossible. I was planning to keep the condo for the nights I work late. You might as well live here. In a few months the house should be finished, and I'll be moving out of the city, anyway. Until then we can figure out who gets the bed and who gets the sofa."

Her eyes clouded briefly. "Sure?"

He knew this particular insecurity well, and said casually, "Positive. But on one condition. This time unpack and spread out. Last time you came you kept your stuff in your suitcase stuck in the closet for two weeks. If you're going to live here, live here. Okay?"

"Okay. Thanks." Her shoulders relaxed. "The house is that close to being finished, huh?"

"Yeah, it's coming along great. You can come and help me tomorrow, if you like." He noticed her sleepy eyes and smiled. "Since you had the bed last, why don't you finish the night there? I'll take the sofa. We can work out our sleeping arrangements tomorrow."

"I'm not sleepy. How about hot chocolate?"

"I don't have any."

"Yes, you do. I bought groceries on my way here." She unfurled her long, long legs and stood. Luke rose at the same time, and they came nose-to-nose, inches apart.

He'd forgotten how tall she was. Her mouth was almost on a level with his.

If he bent his knees...

If Cat stood on her toes...

If she had been any other desirable woman, he would have slipped his arms about her slender waist, drawn her against his chest and kissed that soft succulent mouth until they were both gasping for air. He quickly shook off the thought.

He trailed her into his chrome-and-black-glass kitchen, observing the way her hips moved as she padded on bare feet. She had a loose-jointed walk that made Playboy centerfolds look like windup toys.

Luke settled at the small table under the window as Cat heated milk and made their drinks. She knew where everything was because she'd put it there when he'd moved in two years ago.

"Thanks." Luke took the brimming mug she offered. Chocolate-scented steam tantalized his taste buds. He waited until she slid into the other chair before he spoke. "You were stifled in that house with Dad all those years, Cat. I understand you wanting to try something new and exciting. And San Francisco certainly is that. But don't you think it might be a culture shock?"

She'd taken a tentative sip and already wore a chocolate milk mustache. She watched him over the rim of her mug. Transfixed, he watched her pink tongue come out and lick the creamy film off her upper lip. He was going to drop dead from a heart attack at age thirty-three.

Her eyes flickered away, then back again.

"Okay, Cat. What are you up to?"

"Me?" She was all wide-eyed innocence. "Nothing."

"The first time you gave me that look was when you said you weren't running away to join the circus, remember? We found you in the park two blocks away, panhandling for bus fare."

Cat grinned. "I promise, I don't want to join the circus."

The chocolate must have burned the hell out of her throat, but she chugged it down, then cradled the empty mug. She had pretty hands. Slender, no-nonsense, with short, unpolished nails. He wanted them on him.

Luke's heart took up an unexpected arrhythmic beat as he watched her. Despite her mother's influence, Cat had always been a sensible woman. Somehow she'd remained refreshingly innocent. She was what was known as a "good girl." More than likely the last of a dying breed. In spite of her lush, curvy body, she was wholesome. Natural.

Cat gave him a level, serious look. "I came because you're the only man I trust, Luke. I have a problem."

He felt sick. "Do you want him to marry you, or do you want me to punch him out?"

Cat looked at him blankly. "Marry? Punch? Who?"

"Cat, for God's sake! The man who got you pregnant!"

She stared at him as though he'd lost his mind. "I'm a virgin, Luke."

"Well, hell, what does that have to do with anyth— What?"

"Virgin? Unmarried woman? Untouched? Pure?"

"Jesus." His breath gusted out, and it took several moments to get his heartbeat back to comfortable. He scraped his fingers through his hair, feeling ridiculously as if he'd stood perilously close to the edge of an abyss and survived. "Sorry, I tend to get a little carried away," he admitted gruffly.

"I've noticed." Cat's voice was dry. Her mouth wore a small, tentative smile, but her eyes still looked as if she were about to tell him something he didn't want to hear. He'd anticipated the worst and rallied. Relaxing, he leaned back in his chair.

"What do you need help with? Want to come and work out of our office? No problem, I told you we'll find a spot for you—"

She watched him with big, serious eyes. "I don't want you to find me office space, Luke. I want you to find me a husband."

2

"WELL, SAY SOMETHING." Catherine tried not to let her nerves show as he sat there gaping.

Even while she'd agonized over doing this, she'd hoped she'd have to go no further than to ask Luke for his help. It would have made life a whole bunch easier if he'd just cut to the chase and declared his undying love for her at the onset.

The Plan hadn't gotten much beyond that. She wanted more, but with Luke's attitude toward permanence, she was realistic enough to know she wasn't going to get it.

Her biggest leap of faith had been to burn her bridges, and take the chance that he wouldn't reject her outright. Again.

Ten years was a long time, she kept reminding herself. They'd both grown up since. She wasn't that naive, impulsive kid anymore. She knew Luke better now. For her plan to work, this seduction was going to have to be his idea. Unfortunately, he was still staring at her, slack-jawed.

"Well?" she said with a shaky breath. "Say something."

"I'm speechless."

"Could you hurry up and get over it?" Catherine pulled a yellow scratch pad and a pen out of the canvas bag she'd slung over the finial of her chair earlier. She concentrated on writing "Prospective Husbands" at the top of the page in neat block letters, more to give Luke time to assimilate what she'd said than the need to make a list. She glanced up. His eyes were squinty.

"What?" she asked innocently.

"What do you mean, you want me to find you a husband? You have a phobic aversion to marriage!"

"No. That's you." *Keep it casual, Catherine.* "I have a phobic aversion to my mother's marriages. What if poor marital judgment is hereditary? My apple might have fallen closer to my mother's tree than I'd like. I just don't trust my own judgment."

"And you'd trust mine? I don't believe in marriage, remember?"

How could she forget? "You'll meet someone someday."

"No," he said unequivocally. "I won't. And frankly, Cat, considering we've both seen your mother in action, I'm surprised that you'd want to make the same mistakes."

"With your help, I won't."

"I don't get it. Why?"

"Because I need someone to take care of, Luke. After Dad died I realized I liked taking care of someone. I love being a homemaker. I know it's politically incorrect not to want a career, but I don't. I enjoy trading stocks on the market, and as long as I have my computer and a phone line, I can do that anywhere. But if I had to stop that tomorrow, I wouldn't care. I guess I'm a throwback, what can I say? I want a husband to love, and to be loved by. Eventually kids. I want a couple of dogs, and a house with a big yard. Is that too much to ask—where are you going?"

"To make more hot chocolate."

"There's still some. Here." She handed him her mug and waited while he poured hot chocolate haphazardly from the pan. Catherine observed the motion of muscles flexing beneath his green sweater. She drew in a deep breath, then held it until her stomach behaved itself. Luke had never made any bones about his intention to remain a bachelor. She remembered him telling her just that, right after his own mother remarried for the third time. Luke didn't believe in promises any more than Catherine did. The difference was she was willing to take the chance. Luke wasn't.

He yanked open a cabinet and grabbed a bottle of something hideously expensive, using more force than necessary. She perked up. Wrenching the cap off, he sloshed liquor into his mug, then slammed the bottle onto the black granite countertop. Even better.

"Are we celebrating?" she asked as he placed both mugs on the table. She plucked napkins out of the holder to mop up the chocolate milk he'd sloshed onto the tabletop.

"What do you think, Catherine?" He strode back to retrieve the liquor bottle, which he slam-dunked onto the table between them. Then, scowling, he threw himself into his chair and raked his fingers through his hair until it stood up like a shark fin.

"Well, I think a celebration is a little premature right now...but sure." She reached out to take the bottle. Luke removed it gently from her grasp. Which was fine with her. If it tasted anything like it smelled, she'd gag. *Come on, Luke,* she silently urged, *let's hear it.*

"Are you out of your mind, Cat?" A vein throbbed in his temple. His eyes had turned a smoky green. "If you have this burning need to take care of something, get a poodle."

"Not quite the same thing, Luke."

Even with that look of total exasperation on his face he was the sexiest man she'd ever laid eyes on. Too sexy for plain Catherine Harris. But she wanted him anyway. Her and about a billion other women. Luke Van Buren was Mr. Confirmed Bachelor Playboy himself. He'd never had to look for female companionship. Anything female would spot him from a hundred feet away and be charmed. He loved women. He treated his girlfriends with care and consideration, and adored them.

As long as he was with them.

Lucas Van Buren epitomized the expression "out of sight, out of mind." Over the years she'd witnessed the ebb and flow of Luke's lady friends. None of the relationships lasted very long. Which didn't bode well for her own future. But if she didn't try, how would she ever know?

Luke was a freewheeling playboy. She valued security and stability above all else. He was a daredevil who considered variety the spice of life. She wanted marriage. He wanted affairs.

She wanted him. He didn't want her.

When she'd first decided to come to San Francisco she'd considered asking Luke to find her a lover, not a husband. Since he wasn't husband material, that would have been closer to the truth. But she'd immediately dismissed that idea. Luke would have choked out a resounding and unequivocal "N.O."

"Did being stuck in that house with just Dad for company turn your gray matter into oatmeal?"

"Not that I know of. Look, this is quite simple, Luke. You must know a gazillion single guys. Lots of cultures have marriage brokers. Which, if you think about it, makes perfect sense. Look at the divorce rate when people find mates by random selection. It's up to sixty percent. Our mothers probably had a lot to do with that figure rising."

He splashed more amber liquid into his mug. His knuckles glowed white where he gripped the bottle. He hadn't said a word in minutes.

"You're intelligent. You know me, you care about me. You'll make a perfect marriage broker. Pick a few friends you think would make good husband material and I'll do the rest."

Catherine grabbed the pen, ignored the thud of her heartbeat right under her breastbone, and gave him a perky smile. She set the tip of the pen in the left margin and wrote a large number one. "Any interesting prospects in your address book under *A*?"

HE'D DONE SOMETHING really bad in another life and God was punishing him, Luke thought as he silently opened the bedroom door several sleepless hours later. To get to the bathroom and a cold shower, he had to traverse the bedroom where Cat slept. He'd spent a miserable night on the sofa thinking about her—and her harebrained scheme.

The world was her oyster. She should be enjoying the bliss of singlehood. Besides, how could a woman whose mother had been married at last count, eight times, even consider marriage?

Variety was the spice of life. Why would anyone put all their emotional eggs in one basket? How could one person be everything to another person? It wasn't logical. It wasn't smart. And Cat was usually so sensible, so predictable, so...sane.

Last night she'd been too tired to listen to reason. He'd talk some sense into her today, he decided, as he sneaked into his own sun-washed bedroom on Sunday morning, averting his gaze from the bed—for half a heartbeat.

Sleeping the sleep of the innocent and still wearing his sweatshirt, Cat sprawled diagonally across his California King mattress, sunlight streaming across her smooth bare legs. His fingers itched to slide up the satiny expanse. He wanted to follow his hands with his mouth and taste those freckles.

He sped into the bathroom, closed the door and wilted against it in his relief to have made it this far unscathed.

An icy shower went a long way to making him feel halfway human. When he opened the bathroom door again the first thing he saw was Cat's smiling face. His heart did a ridiculous and wholly inappropriate double axel as she sat up in bed, his bed, to smile at him.

"Good morning." She yawned, stretching like a cat.

"Get your lazy butt out of bed, woman," he told her sternly, digging through the chaos of his drawers for clean underwear while he held on to the towel around his waist with the other hand. "We have things to do and places to go." He'd have to knuckle down and do laundry soon. He looked over his shoulder and raised an eyebrow at her. "Are you awake in there?"

Cat shook her head as if to clear it, then scrambled over the edge of the bed. "You betcha, Bubba. Give me ten minutes and I'm all yours." She shuffled into the bathroom. The door snicked behind her. He dropped the towel, dragged on underwear over damp skin and waited for the click of the lock.

He waited in vain.

The shower turned on.

He struggled to zip his jeans.

The bedroom smelled like Cat. Soft. Flowery. Permanent. He searched the upper shelves for a sweat-shirt. Finding one he'd stuffed in there months ago, he held it up. Not too wrinkled. So he put it on.

"Hey, Luke?" she shouted over the noise of pounding water.

He closed his eyes. "What?"

"Did you come up with some names for me?" The shower turned off. "Hey. What happened to the towe—never mind, found them."

People showered naked every day of the week. He wished to hell Cat wasn't one of them. "We'll talk about it."

"What? I can't hear... That's better." A billow of Cat-scented steam preceded her as she opened the door. "Well, did you?"

"I said..." he clenched his teeth, bending down to tie the laces on his boots. They were on the wrong feet. He removed, then switched them, before tackling the laces. "...we'll talk about it."

She came out of the bathroom wearing one towel around her body, another wrapped turban style about her head. Her face was scrubbed shiny, her skin like fresh cream sprinkled with cinnamon. Her legs went on forever. In his fantasies he joined the dots.

If she was any other woman... But she was Cat. He'd bite off his own foot before he'd hurt her. This was not a woman a man played with. Cat was a keeper.

There wasn't a drop of blood in common between them. Their relationship was a state of mind. One he'd better keep remembering. She thought of him as her *brother*, he reminded himself grimly. Therefore Cat was off-limits. A no-no. Absolutely forbidden fruit.

"I hope it'll be soon, Luke." She pulled the towel from her head. "I'm not getting any younger, you know."

"Who is?" He'd tied the laces too tight, but he walked to the door anyway. When he turned back he managed to look just at her hair. Wet and wild, it tangled around her face and bare shoulders, and lovingly clung, like wet flames, to the upper swell of her—

"Hurry up and dress, will you? It's past ten and my stomach thinks my throat's been cut."

He closed the door gently behind him, feeling as though he'd just escaped something too terrifying to contemplate.

"OH, MY GOD, LUKE, don't take the corners so fast!" Catherine screamed as the Hideous Harley did a faster-than-a-speeding-bullet skim around another corner. Clinging to his waist, she gripped his belt buckle with both hands. The seat felt obscenely wide between her thighs.

"Lean, Cat. Lean."

She leaned, sure her helmet must have brushed the gray asphalt as they cornered at an impossible angle.

Luke hadn't given her time to dry her hair. The moment she'd dressed in jeans and another of his oversize sweatshirts, he'd hustled her down to the parking garage, ignored his well-preserved 1977 Jag, climbed onto his enormous black demon motorcycle, handed her the spare helmet, revved the engine and instructed her to hold on.

If she'd been holding him any tighter, she would have been in front. The speed scared her speechless, no easy feat. Nevertheless, she'd better learn to love the wind tugging her hair from the helmet, biting into her face and making her nose and eyes run. Luke loved his bike.

His house was an hour south of San Francisco, down narrow, windy, stomach-churning coastal roads. Catherine squeezed her eyes shut and buried her icy nose against his leather-clad back, remembering the first time he'd taken her up behind him. She'd been ten. He was seventeen.

He'd only taken her because Dad had insisted she get the first ride on his new bike. She'd been terrified. Luke had been furious at her for being such a baby and had screamed blue murder at her for three blocks. The wind had caused her eyes to tear. And Luke and Dad had had a huge, yelling, door-slamming fight when they got back.

"Loosen up a bit, Catwoman. I can't breath."

Since Catherine hadn't drawn a proper breath in more than an hour, she ignored his request. He felt warm and solid in her arms. "Are we there yet?" she whined like a five-year-old.

She felt Luke's laugh vibrate through her body like dark, sinfully rich chocolate. Oh, yes. She'd made the right decision coming to San Francisco. Yes, indeedy.

"STOP HERE FOR A SEC," Catherine demanded an hour later as the bike turned from the tarred road parallel to the ocean onto the as-yet-unpaved gravel of Luke's new driveway. The fog had burned off, leaving sparkling spring sunshine glinting off the Pacific in the distance. Catherine inhaled the fresh briny air deep into her lungs as she let go of him and flung her leg over the bike the moment he brought it to a stop.

She stood, took off her helmet, then shaded her eyes with one hand against the sun, waiting for her heart to take up its normal rhythm after being glued to Luke for miles.

While the soft whoosh of the ocean sounded behind her, she forced herself to check out his house, as opposed to analyzing which body part felt what from the close encounter of the third kind with Luke's body.

Constructed of weathered redwood, tucked into the surrounding trees on a bluff overlooking a sliver of beach and the vastness of the ocean, the single-story house already had a look of permanence. Wonderfully gnarled, windblown cypress trees dotted the front yard.

"It's going to be magnificent, Luke."

Unaccountably, she felt the sting of tears, and rubbed the end of her nose with her palm. The house had been a goal of his for as long as she could remember. From the second he'd decided he wanted to be an architect, Luke had vowed to build his house from the ground up with his own two hands. A strangely permanent idea for a temporary kind of guy. Catherine wondered if Luke realized how at odds owning a house was with his playboy lifestyle.

While Luke loved the intricate curlicues and elaborate bits and pieces of Victorian houses, he'd explained to her once that he needed the clean, uncluttered lines of more modern architecture to cleanse his palate when he came home.

She noticed the enormous bay window in the living room. A window she'd suggested one rainy winter's night as they'd poured over the first version of his blueprints years ago. She doubted if he suspected how many of her own dreams had been woven into his house plans.

Gravel crunched under his workboots as Luke came up behind her and rested his hands lightly on her shoulders. They stood silently for several moments looking up the slight incline to the house. Catherine was excruciatingly conscious of him behind her. She felt each finger on her shoulders, the warmth of his tall body shielding her back from the hair-ruffling breeze. The air smelled of salt spray and fresh lumber. But most of all it smelled of sun-warmed Luke in leather.

His proximity had already caused her stomach to coil into knots. After an hour of straddling his rangy body she needed to put some distance between them.

She stepped out of reach and smiled over her shoulder. "Let's walk the rest of the way so we can get the full ambiance."

Luke grimaced and Catherine grinned. If Luke could ride instead of walk, sit instead of stand or call instead of write, he was a happy man.

"Exercise is good for you. It can't be more than half a mile."

"These are workboots," he told her, "not walking boots. I have to save my energy for bossing you and Nick around."

She shrugged. "Fine. I'll walk. You ride. You should be an interesting looking specimen once you hit forty. Flabby. Weak. Pasty. Probably sickly. That's okay," she said cheerfully, "you won't be the first man to wear a waist cincher."

Luke sighed, then knocked back the kickstand with his toe and rolled the bike beside her. "I go to the gym four times a week."

Catherine laughed. "You go there to pick up women." Luke's indolence had been a family joke. Yet there'd been nothing soft about the stomach muscles she'd felt when she'd clung to him on the bike, or the hard, tight muscles in his behind pressed between her thighs. There wasn't a flabby muscle on Luke's six-three frame.

"I pay the dues. I can do whatever I want."

He probably bench-pressed two blond gym bunnies. He might give the impression of being lazy, but Luke was no slouch in the flirtation department. Catherine had seen him in action. How many women, despite knowing Luke's views on marriage, wanted him anyway? But she wasn't going to dwell on that today. She was the woman he was with on this beautiful spring day. And she was going to enjoy every moment of it.

On either side of the slightly rolling topography, weeds, shrubs and vines tangled with thick trunks of oak, pine and cypress. There wasn't another house for half a mile. The only sounds were ocean breezes and insects in the long grasses.

"Nick's late," Luke commented as he detoured to angle the monster bike through a patch of sand, parking it against a prefab shed off to one side of the half-finished front porch.

"You work the poor guy like a slave. We barely got here ourselves."

"He's cheap, but he's good." Luke squinted in the wind that ruffled his dark hair. He sent her a grin. "And he's bringing lunch. Now, if I could just get him to give up some of his active social life, I might have this house finished next month as planned."

"It's a long commute," she said casually. A month? My God, there was no way she could pull this off in a month. Could she?

"Well, the office won't be practically across the street as it is now, but an hour's commute these days is nothing. Come on, I want to show off everything before Nick gets here."

Catherine followed Luke slowly as he walked up the wide, shallow redwood steps onto a deep porch. He bounced lightly, testing each tread. His fingers lingered as he trailed them up the simple banister beside the front steps. He took pride in his craftsmanship and it showed. Luke had a hedonistic pleasure in textures.

He always had. She was jealous of the attention the wood was getting.

Catherine swallowed hard, remembering the night of her dateless junior prom. Luke had come to spend that weekend with his father. Exuberant as always, he'd burst into her room and found her crying. He hadn't known what to do with a weepy female, and had plucked the hairbrush out of her hand. More, she'd been sure, for something to do with his hands than to console her, he'd ended up brushing her hair for hours as they talked. Luke looking at the back of her head, Catherine watching his face, unobserved, in her vanity mirror across the room. She never did remember what they'd talked about, only that it was the first time she'd experienced sexual awareness. For her, it was the night their relationship had changed forever.

That was the night she'd realized she loved him.

Her ponytail brushed between her shoulder blades and she shivered, remembering the sensual pleasure of Luke's fingers in her hair, against her nape.... *Get a grip here*, she warned herself sternly, as she waited for him to unlock the massive oak door. Before she followed him inside, she bent to pull a weed that had managed to grow through the wood slats.

"Gonna plant that in a pot?" Luke turned, indicating the two-foot weed clutched in her hand, soil trailing from its roots.

His smile tangled up in Catherine's heart. Sunlight stroked his dark hair and magnified his strong, unshaved jaw. His long, lean body looked breathtaking in washed-almost-white jeans and a short leather jacket. He looked handsome, disreputable and too sexy for a small-town girl from Oregon. Yet she wanted him more than her next breath. She held out the droopy weed. "Got a pot?"

"And a window," he said dryly. "Here, give me that. I'll take you on the twenty-dollar tour." He took the plant, tossed it outside, then brushed off his hands.

"Twenty bucks, huh?"

"And worth every penny. Careful where you walk. Not all the nails are countersunk in the subflooring."

The square entry echoed their footsteps as she followed him into a large room filled with sawhorses, paint cans, lumber scraps and other paraphernalia of construction. Sunlight streamed through the plastic-covered windows. The room smelled of fresh wood, mudding compound and dust. She sidestepped boxes of nails and a mountain of Sheetrock to cross the room.

"Wow. This fireplace looks great." Catherine ran her hand lightly over the enormous natural stones, then glanced at him over her shoulder. "Did you carry even one of these monstrous rocks?"

He gave her a horrified look as he removed his jacket, tossing it onto a stepladder. "Are you kidding? What do you think Nick is for? Poor spindly fellow, he needed the exercise."

Catherine shook her head. "You're terrible. What was the bet?"

"Who could eat the most soft pretzels." He puffed out his chest, stretching his black T-shirt over hard muscle. Catherine's mouth went dry. "I ate twenty-three."

"Gross. You must have been sick as a dog."

"Well, yeah. But it was worth it." His grin was infectious and her heart leaped ridiculously as he laid his arm across her shoulders and stood beside her, looking at the wall of stone with pride. "There are over two hundred fieldstones imbedded in that thar li'l ol' fireplace."

Reaching to the cathedral ceiling, and about fifteen feet wide, it hardly qualified as little. She shook her head, used to Luke's and Nick's ridiculous but harmless bets.

"When are you two going to stop that nonsense? You've been betting on anything and everything since fifth grade."

"We did a sealed bet when we'd stop."

Catherine shook her head again and slipped casually from under his arm. The back of her neck tingled and her knees felt wobbly as she strolled over to the plastic-covered bay window.

"Oh, Luke, this is absolutely glorious. Look at this view. Are there any deer out there, do you think?"

"Several. I saw a doe and her fawn last weekend."

He walked over and leaned against an exposed stud, his arms folded as he watched her from hooded eyes. *A stud leaning against a stud. How appropriate.* Uncomfortable under his scrutiny, she shifted without looking at him.

"Are you okay?"

"Of course," she said brightly. "Why wouldn't I be?"

"You just seem...I don't know...different."

"Different? How?" Since when?

"I don't know." He looked as puzzled as he sounded.

Excruciatingly aware of him watching her, she didn't know where to look, what to do with her too-large hands and feet.

"There's Nick! Is that his new car? I'll go out and help him carry whatever he's brought for lunch."

If she took a breath in there, Luke didn't hear it. She dashed out of the room, fiery ponytail bobbing against her shoulders, her sneakers echoing in the vast, empty room. Luke stared at her retreating back, avoiding the view of her tight little butt in retreat.

He shook his head and followed her outside. Just in time to see her fling herself into Nick's open arms.

Scowling, Luke jogged down the stairs, gave a cursory glance at the screaming red BMW parked beside his bike, and dug into his back pocket. When Nick caught his eye over Cat's head, Luke flashed him the twenty in his hand. The top of Cat's head reached Nick's jaw. Luke didn't like the way they had their arms looped about each other's waist as they strolled toward the house together.

He'd seen that look in his partner's eye about seven million times. Luke wanted to gently set Cat aside and pummel his best friend's and business partner's face into the dirt. Twice, for good measure. He settled for a meaningful glare.

Nick grinned. Still holding Cat under one brawny arm, he snagged the money out of Luke's fingers. "Thank you kindly, son." He chuckled, stuffing the bill into his front pocket.

Cat glanced from one to the other and raised one red eyebrow.

"License plate. Has two threes in it," Luke explained, keeping abreast with them on the steps and porch, but unable to squeeze through the front door. He glared at Nick, whose mockingbird-blue eyes held the devil today.

All three of them paused on the threshold.

"We could try it single file," Cat offered seriously, her head doing the tennis match waltz to see who was going to cave first.

"No," Luke and Nick agreed. Nick pulled a quarter out of his pocket. "Call it."

"Tails."

The coin caught the light as it twisted in the air, then landed on Nick's palm. "Step back, pardner. The lady's with me tonight."

Luke scowled as he followed them into the living room. There wasn't that much heavy lifting to do. He could have done without Nick's help today.

3

"Well, honey, aren't you absolutely, outrageously gorgeous?" Nick released Catherine's waist, only to capture both her hands. He held her in front of him, arms spread wide, their fingers entwined, as he checked her out from head to toe, and all ports in between. She gave him a frank stare back. She'd adored him for almost twenty years. Almost as long as she'd known Luke. It puzzled her why, when Nick was a truly delicious hunk of manhood, she'd never felt any of the sparks that ignited at just the thought of Luke.

"In eight months," she teased, "I had two more calls from you than I did from Luke. I had to come and see for myself if you guys were behaving yourselves."

"I gotta tell you, sweet thing, if I'd known you'd get even more beautiful, I would've called three times a day."

Catherine pulled her hands free and gave him a mild look. "Three times a day, huh? What on earth would we talk about?"

"Your fantastic hair." Nick reached out and fingered a few strands near her face, then lowered his smoky voice. "Your skin, your eyes, your mouth—"

"Hey, Stratton, give it a rest. Cat's immune to your dubious charms."

Although Catherine felt the pulse of Luke's presence

in the room, she managed to ignore him and to encourage Nick. "More. More."

Nick's answering grin revealed two long, sexy dimples in his lean cheeks. His dark hair had a tendency to curl. He kept it cut short, reminding her of the profile on a Greek coin. He was a clotheshorse, and his tall, spare body looked good in whatever he wore. Today he'd dressed in Dockers, his only concession to work a pair of immaculate workboots. His lavender golf shirt made his blue eyes look violet.

He grinned wickedly at Luke. "We're going to have to keep Princess under lock and key while she's visiting, won't we?"

"I'm not visiting." Catherine pushed his hand away from her hair, which he'd been absently fondling. "Dragon over there is letting me stay with him until the house is ready."

Nick stuck his hands in his pockets and gave Luke a level look. "Is that so?"

"I'm not going to be moving in before the turn of the century unless you two get to work," Luke told them shortly, dropping the last torn piece of sandpaper he'd been shredding to join the others at his feet. He cast Nick a mildly belligerent look.

"Please tell me my portfolio is still in your capable hands?" Nick begged with utmost sincerity. Four of Catherine's savvy trades had made his new Beemer possible.

"Safe and sound," she assured him. "Boy, I'd kill for a cup of coffee." She edged past Luke, who didn't like losing and was obviously still smarting over two losses in one morning. "Guys?"

The men followed her into the kitchen. The oak cabinets had been installed and gleamed in the sun streaming through the plastic over the kitchen window opening. The naked plywood countertops looked ready for tile. A card table shoved into the refrigerator opening held a coffeepot and several sealed jars. A commercial water bottle sat on the floor under the table. Catherine set about making coffee as Luke divvied up the assignments for the day.

"Plan on taking a *short* break," Luke warned his helpers. "Here." He handed her a how-to-install-tile book. "Bone up on this while you finish your coffee."

"You're trusting me to do this after glancing at a book?"

Luke shrugged. "How could a compulsive personality screw up?"

Catherine pulled a face. "Let me count the ways." She tucked the book under her arm. "You're nuts, but I'm game. Gimme my supplies, boss."

"Get your coffee first, and I'll stick what you need in the bathroom down the hall." Luke accepted the brimming paper cup Catherine handed him. "Yo, Nick? Did you say you brought lunch?"

Nick went out to his car to retrieve the cooler while Luke showed Catherine what needed to be done in the guest bathroom.

"You're not going to stay in here and watch, are you?" Catherine sucked in her stomach to make room for him to maneuver around her in the compact bathroom. With a neat knee bend, he set the box of tiles he carried on the floor. Catherine averted her eyes from his crotch. He looked up. Their eyes met and she blushed. She could've sworn she saw an answering heat in his eyes. But then, it was pretty dim in here. Much to her embarrassment, she'd mistaken that look before.

"Nick hasn't gotten involved with anyone in the last couple of weeks, has he?" she asked, hoping to redirect her thoughts.

Luke rose slowly. "Why do you want to know?"

She laughed. "Gee, let me think. He's tall, dark, handsome, owns his own business, is single and has most of his own teeth."

"He owns half a business, and he's the last man you should be looking at." Luke bent to retrieve a large can of mastic from beneath the sink and used a screwdriver from his back pocket to open it. It smelled noxious. "You know Nick'll never commit."

"So? I like him."

"Good." Luke slapped a notched trowel down beside the can. "So do I. Let's keep it that way."

Catherine leaned against the doorjamb with her arms folded. Willpower kept her voice even as a bubble of laughter caught in her throat. "Talk about the pot calling the kettle black!"

"Would you move...thanks." His sleeve brushed her chest as he maneuvered past her to the door. "Think you can handle this, or would you rather paint?"

"I'd rather talk about Nick."

"Yell if you get stuck."

Catherine heard his workboots pound down the hall to the kitchen. She grinned.

"I SEE NO END OF PROBLEMS if she stays with me indefinitely," Luke said morosely over his shoulder as he and Nick installed custom milled molding in the master suite. "Why couldn't she have stayed in Beaverton where she belongs?"

Nick, standing on the ladder, took a few whacks with a hammer as he drove a nail into the twelve-inch-wide oak. "By herself?"

"She has friends there." Luke said, then hammered a few finishing nails into the baseboard. "And she sold the house."

"It's not like Catherine to burn her bridges. She means to stick around, I guess."

"She asked me to help her find a husband."

Nick's teeth flashed in a devilish grin. "Whose?"

Luke snorted. "That's the problem. Everyone we know is just like us."

"What's wrong with us? We're good-looking, own our own business, have decent cars and can flash the cash." He twisted on the ladder to look down at Luke.

Luke hadn't liked the way Nick's eyes had danced the moment he'd seen Cat this morning. He didn't like the way his best friend had kept his arm wrapped about Cat's slender waist, either. He gave Nick a pointed look.

"She's got great girl parts," Nick said with far too much enthusiasm. "I'd be more than happy to take her out."

"Don't you suddenly start ogling her parts," Luke warned. "Everything from the neck down is strictly off-limits."

"Her lips are fair game?"

"Consider her verboten from head to toe, and all

parts in between. Does Cat look desperate for a date? She wants a lifetime commitment. Someone stable. Faithful. A guy who'll see no one but her. You aren't even on the *D* list of candidates."

"Do you have an *A* list?" Nick asked, amused.

"You and I are going to work on it," Luke said with grim determination. "At first I tried to talk her out of it. But you know Cat. Once she's set on something she's like a pit bull."

"More like I know *you*," Nick said. "When Catherine wants something, *you* bend over backward to make sure she gets it."

"She's never asked for much, and she deserves to be happy. I'm hoping it'll be a case of be careful what you wish for. So...how many of our friends fit the 'decent-guy, keeps-his-hands-to-himself, faithful' description?"

"Catherine's a beautiful, intelligent woman. She must've been kidding about finding her a husband," Nick said. "Why would a woman who looks like she does, and makes money hand over fist, want to tie herself down to one guy? She'll have to beat men off with a two-by-four as soon as word gets around she's available."

"I prefer she do it in Oregon." Luke stood, dusting off his jeans. "I'm starving."

The bathroom door was almost closed as they walked by. "Hey, Cat." Luke rapped on the door. "Ready for lunch?" She was on her knees behind the door. He could just see her endearingly large feet poking out.

"Yeah, I'm famished. Almost finished here. Go

ahead and start without me. Hey! Make sure you guys leave something edible."

"See, that's the problem," Luke said, picking up their conversation as they entered the kitchen. He dragged the lid off the cooler Nick had left on the counter earlier. "It's gonna be impossible finding someone whose intentions are halfway honorable. Do you want tuna or...what's this? Mystery meat? Here, take it, whatever it is."

Nick removed the wrapping and raised his roast beef sandwich to his mouth. "Tell her you don't want her here."

Luke sent his friend a level look. "I can't do that again, Nick. You know that. I have a history of telling Cat she's not wanted. Prince of a guy that I am, I started the day her mother left..." Luke scrubbed his jaw. "She cried herself sick for four days."

"She was seven years old."

"Yeah. And that was the last time I saw her cry. Think of all the times she *didn't* cry when I embarrassed her by telling my friends I didn't even know her. That was even worse."

"Give yourself a break. You were a teenager. She followed you around school like a sad-eyed puppy. Hey, *I* told her to bug off on more than one occasion."

"She used to scrunch up under that berry bush way in the back of the middle school playground, remember the one? Just scrunch up under all those thorns after I'd told her to get lost. I'd walk by and see her, and feel lower than the scales on a snake's belly. That sad little face, and all that crazy red hair. And she refused to cry. I could see she wanted to, but damn her stubborn pride, she refused. And I'd walk away, laughing with my friends, and leave her there."

Nick bit into his three-inch-thick sandwich, catching the sliced pickle before it hit his boot. He stuffed it back between the slices of bread, then licked mustard off his thumb. "And then there's her seventeenth birthday."

Luke's head shot up. "Don't go there, Stratton."

Oblivious to the danger, Nick continued. "You kissed her, she puked. End of story. Fine. She's a big girl now, odds are she doesn't still throw up when a man kisses her. But who knows? Why take the risk of her upchucking on a friend? Hey, I'm sure she'll understand if you tell her to get lost. After all, as you say, been there, done that, got the scars to prove it. Besides, just about everyone in Catherine's life has abandoned her. Why should you be any different?"

Luke closed his eyes. He hadn't told Nick more than the basics. The truth was he'd allowed his passions to get away from him that night, and in the process had scared Cat to death. She'd needed her *brother*. Instead he'd turned into Octopus Man with suction lips and a hard-on that wouldn't quit.

No wonder she'd been sick. And embarrassed. And disappointed in him. Luke glared at Nick, grateful in a perverse way for the reminder. "It's taken years for her to learn she can trust me again."

The pain he'd caused her by switching roles midstream still tortured him. They'd never talked about that night, but it lay between them like the monster in a misty bog. He'd sworn not only to be her brother, but her hero, her protector. Her champion. In other words, he'd be what Cat needed.

"I've got a lot to make up for. I'm not going to blow it." Luke tossed his uneaten sandwich into the box they used for trash. He wanted to pace, but that took up too much energy, so he leaned against the counter.

"Got a beer in here?" He dug through the ice and pulled out two cans. "Hey, Cat?" he shouted, handing Nick a beer. "Come and get it."

He waited a beat for her faint answer, then popped the can and took a long swig. "If she wants help finding a husband, then I'll help her find a husband. Between us, we must know a hundred eligible single guys. Hell, it can't be that difficult."

"Wanna bet?" Nick asked, looking up; his pale blue eyes weren't smiling as he issued the age-old refrain. Polishing off his sandwich, he reached for another. "Engagement or wedding?"

Luke narrowed his eyes. Man. He hated this whole situation. "Wedding, I guess."

"Four months."

"Six. Payoff?"

"Milk in my oldest gym shoe?" Nick asked seriously.

"Get real, Stratton! This is Cat we're talking about here."

"Aah! A Major Bet. Mmm," Nick rubbed his chin. "An all-expenses-paid trip to Vegas. For two."

They shook on it.

"I'm ECSTATIC TO ANNOUNCE the toilet in the master bath flushes," Catherine said to the room in general. She stumbled into the kitchen, then her knees folded and she sat down in the middle of the floor with a thump.

"First order of business—" Luke broke off abruptly as he turned from the window. "You look like hell. What's wrong with you?"

"Your bathroom made me sick."

At the speed of light, Luke came down on one knee in front of her. "How sick?" He pushed her hair off her clammy forehead.

Catherine gave him a look. "Barf sick."

He rose, scooping her into his arms. *Very manly,* Catherine thought as he strode through the house, yelling for Nick to open the damn front door. She rested her throbbing head on his nicely muscled shoulder and closed her eyes to stop the world spinning.

"Take a couple of deep breaths," Luke demanded, stomping to the edge of the porch and sitting down on the top step. Right, like she could draw a breath while sitting on Lucas Van Buren's lap.

"Cat? Breathe, dammit."

She took a shuddery breath. His splayed hand on her rib cage moved with her lungs. She tried it again. It felt good. She couldn't figure out now if she was still dizzy from the glue or if it was Luke's touch making her head spin.

Catherine squinted her eyes open as Nick settled himself on the other end of the step and leaned against the post, a beer can in one hand. He gave her a small, one-dimple smile. "Glue?" he asked Luke, swallowing his amusement with a gulp of brew.

Luke's hand slipped a fraction of an inch down her rib cage as his breath fanned the top of her head. He was probably getting a mouthful of her unruly hair. His hand shifted up again. *Up,* Catherine silently ordered. *Move up more.*

"Fool woman, I told her to open the window."

"The one you painted closed last weekend?" Nick asked.

"Why didn't she say so?" Luke's chest huffed under her cheek. His hand was directly under her right breast. If he'd just move his thumb...

"Perhaps because you weren't listening when she *did* tell you." Catherine joined in the conversation. "Nevertheless, she is a big girl, and should have figured out a way to ventilate her workspace." She tilted her head to look up at Luke's very nice chin. "Aren't I squishing you?"

"No."

"The last time I sat on your lap, I was nine." It hadn't felt nearly this good. Or this dangerous. In fact, what she remembered was feeling safe for the first time in living memory.

"You were covered in mud." Luke's voice carried a reminiscent smile.

"You pushed me." They grinned at each other.

Nick rose with a groan. "Oh, bliss, another trip down memory lane. I have molding to finish installing, then I'm outta here."

Luke, as if suddenly realizing the position they were in, slid her unceremoniously off his lap and plopped her on the step next to him. The front door closed behind Nick.

"That was a stupid thing to do," Luke told her. "If

you'd passed out in there, I couldn't have opened the door."

"As much as I thrill at being called stupid, I have to admit I should have thrown my shoe through the window for ventilation. Point taken. Lecture over." She rose, staggered and clutched the roof support. "Oh, ick."

Luke shot up as if someone had lit a firecracker in his back pocket. He grabbed her upper arm and pushed her back down. "That's it. You're useless to me now. I'll never get a lick of work out of you if you keep toppling over and I have to stop what I'm doing to hold you up. You're going home."

THERE WERE EXACTLY twenty-six paces from one wall in his condo to the other. Luke knew. He'd counted them off about nine zillion times. He strode across the living room to glare at the clock near the TV. It was after 1:00 a.m. He'd about worn a path in the carpet. Where in the hell were they?

He cursed taking the Harley to the beach house. With Cat asphyxiated by the damn glue, he'd been afraid she'd fall off the bike coming home. But he hadn't wanted her to go in Nick's brand-spanking-new Beemer, either. Luke did the nine paces from the wall unit to the window like a one-minute mile.

The vertical blinds clattered against the wall as he peered down into the dark street. Unless Cat and Nick were the couple blatantly boinking under the streetlamp on the lawn in the park across the street, they still weren't back. And if they were, he'd kill Nick.

He yanked the cell phone out of his back pocket and

punched redial. It rang. And rang. If they were hiding down on the nineteenth floor, at Nick's place, his business partner–ex-best friend was dead meat. Luke slammed the phone off and into his pocket midring. He didn't bother with the elevator, he simply jogged the three floors down, then three floors up again.

Irritated that he was so damn irritated, out of breath and out of ideas, Luke threw himself into his favorite chair. The black leather smelled like her and annoyed him even more. He glared at the open front door, willing Cat to walk in before his murder plans were fully hatched.

"ARE YOU SURE we know what you're doing, Nicolas Stratton?" Catherine yawned, barely awake, and rested her head on the padded headrest of Nick's car, her eyes closed. They'd been parked near Fisherman's Wharf, a good two miles from the condo, for an hour and a half.

"You want Luke to see you as a desirable woman, don't you?"

"It's what I've spent the last six hours telling you," she grumbled, rolling her head his way. Catherine opened her eyes. "I want him to see who I am, but I'm scared. What if this doesn't work? God, I couldn't bear losing the relationship we do have."

"Honey, I think you've only thought through part of this plan. Be brave, be daring, be bold. Moving in with him was a smart idea. But what'll really do it is if he has the opportunity to see you through the eyes of someone else. I volunteered. Don't worry, gorgeous, I have the plan well in hand. And my plans always work."

"Yeah," Catherine said, "except when they don't. And Nick? I want you to promise on a stack of Bibles that you'll never tell him how I feel. This has got to be Luke's idea. He has to make the first move."

"This is woman's logic, right? Chase him until he catches you?"

"Basically. Just promise you won't tell. Never. Do you swear?"

"Constantly."

"Nick!"

He crossed his chest in the vicinity of his heart. "I swear I'll never tell Luke how you feel about him."

"Say that so I can believe it. Because I swear to you, Nicolas Stratton, if Luke gets a hint that he's the one I'm trying to catch before I'm ready to tell him, I'll...I'll tell him about you and Babsie."

"That was in twelfth grade."

"Want to bet he won't still be mad?"

"I give you my word," he said with utmost sincerity.

"Good enough." She squinted at the dash clock. "He's probably sleeping, and we're sitting here like idiots in the dead of night, freezing in the car."

"We could've gone for coffee."

"Nick, you're a lunatic, and I adore you. But if I drink one more cup of anything, I'll float away. Please, can I go home now?"

"WHAT ARE YOU DOING?" Catherine cried as Nick picked her up in his arms. The elevator pinged as it stopped on the twenty-second floor. "Nick, you're going to give yourself a hernia carrying me." The doors slid open. He staggered playfully as he strode down the corridor leading to Luke's condo.

"Put your head on my shoulder, your arms around my neck and close your eyes," Nick said softly. "I'm going to give you the opportunity to be a fly on the wall. Hmm, interesting. The front door's wide open."

Catherine looped her arms about his neck and snuggled against Nick's chest. A nice chest. Unfortunately, not Luke's chest.

"Where've you been?"

Ooh. Luke's dragon roar. Catherine kept her eyes closed, her features lax. She imagined flames spewing from his nostrils. This was a good sign. Nick's plan might just work.

"Hey, old son," Nick whispered. "Princess here is sleeping. Lower your tone to a dull bellow, why don'tcha?"

"Why is Cat sleeping?" Luke demanded, with deep suspicion. She could feel the blistering heat of his gaze focused on her.

"You said you wanted to introduce her to some of our...well, let's just say we did a little par-tay-ing."

"I told you to bring her straight home."

"We came straight back."

"Via Hong Kong?"

"We stopped for a bite to eat. Then she wanted a look at my boat."

"For six hours?"

"Gorgeous day for a sail. Look, she's kinda heavy," Nick said over her head. "Mind if I...oh okay, fine, if you want to stand there bitching at me while *you* get the hernia, that's cool."

Luke's arms tightened around her. Bliss. Catherine's head found the natural and perfect hollow beneath his chin. As long as he didn't get that promised hernia, she was content to lie in his arms and enjoy the moment.

"Poor Princess, she needed the break. The last few months have been tough on her."

"She talked to you?" Catherine heard deep suspicion in Luke's voice. His fingers tightened on her upper thigh. "Catherine Harris the clam, the little crab?"

"It's not a state secret, is it?" Nick asked. "Hey, it's great standing here at one-thirty in the morning, in your open doorway shooting the breeze, a comatose woman between us, but how about a drink?"

"I'm only holding her so I don't rearrange that smarmy, pretty-boy face of yours," Luke snarled. "Next time I tell you to bring her right home, you'd better bring her...no, forget it. You keep your grubby paws away from her."

Don't get overexcited, Catherine warned herself as her heart did a little somersault. What she hoped sounded like jealousy might just be Luke in his defensive big-brother mode. But at this point, she'd consider the glass half full.

"Hey, chill. What's your problem? She's over twenty-one and single. You aren't her father."

"No," Luke said grimly over her head. "I'm her brother."

"You aren't that, either," Nick said softly. "Are you, old son?"

4

THIS ENTIRE SITUATION was untenable, Luke swore. How was he going to hide how he felt about Cat?

From her?

From Nick?

From himself?

He'd done it before with some success. But her power was stronger now. He felt himself sailing directly into the Bermuda Triangle at warp speed.

Luke carried her into the dark bedroom, settled her on the bed and heard the front door close behind his ex-best friend.

He pulled off her shoes and tugged the comforter over her, then left the room and stalked back into the kitchen, where he poured a mug of brandy-laced coffee. Morosely, he sat at his small kitchen table and stared at the oil slick on top of the black liquid before reaching for his PalmPilot. The handheld computer was the nineties version of the little black book.

A. Paul Abbott. Brian Andrews.

Luke transferred names into another file labeled PARTY with all the enthusiasm of a man anticipating a train wreck. Robert Kingston. Cy Kronin...Luke paused. The guy had shifty eyes. Really shifty eyes. He deleted Cy's name. Steve Manfield. Good guy. Quiet.

A possible. Bob Nelson? Owned his own company. Had a couple of dogs. A full set of parents...

Luke's folks had been divorced about three years, and he had lived with his mother when Cat and Faith had moved in with his father. He'd disliked both females at first sight. Cat had been tall for her age, with enough wild red hair to cover a small horse, and wall-to-wall freckles. She'd looked sweet, and sad, and a whole lot of trouble. And worst of all, his father had adored her, and Nick thought she was a little doll. His for the taking.

Luke took a swig out of his mug, ashamed as the flood of memories spotlighted his own less than sterling behavior.

Okay, face it. I was jealous as hell back then. He'd been secretly thrilled when, a year later, his father had informed him of his impending divorce. *Good,* Luke had thought with satisfaction. He'd never warmed to Cat's mother, Faith. The irony of her name was not lost on anyone.

There was only one little glitch to Luke's joy at her departure. She'd left behind The Kid.

What kind of mother left a seven-year-old girl with her ex-husband? His father had been delighted. He'd doted on Cat, included her in everything he did. Luke hadn't wanted a sister. He sure hadn't wanted *her.* And he'd told her so in no uncertain terms. On numerous occasions. With all the arrogance of youth, and with no consideration for her feelings.

Later, he realized she'd wanted the same things he had—a father, a mother, a family. To be loved. A place to belong.

Luke felt the sting of shame all over again. To be fair, he'd been a kid himself. He'd felt abandoned and shoved aside. He hadn't, at thirteen, thought or cared about how The Kid felt.

Luke got all the way to the end of his address book. Allan Zukker. Even eliminating those he thought unsuitable for one reason or another, there was still a decent selection. But because the criteria for females wasn't nearly as stringent as those for males, Luke ended up with an unbalanced list—more women than men. Which suited him just fine, except the party wasn't for him. It was for Cat.

He pushed the computer away. He'd even out the list later.

Luke buried his head in his hands. He didn't want the party. He didn't want to introduce Cat to a man who might not appreciate her, might not treat her right. She'd been hurt enough in her life. Cat needed to be loved. Cherished.

Luke pushed his chair back and strode into his living room. Nope. There were no two ways about it. He'd made his bed. Now he had to lie in it. No matter how damn uncomfortable it was. He tossed a pillow and blanket on the black leather sofa and turned out the light.

Yep, he thought, flinging himself down on his back, fully clothed. He was going to have to bite the bullet and help Cat find the man of her dreams.

Even if it killed him.

THE PARTY WAS A ROARING success. At the moment, E.L.O.'s "Don't Bring Me Down" was competing with raised voices and the din of heels on bare wood floors. Cat had rolled up the area rugs for dancing.

Earlier they'd gone into a cooking frenzy, each trying to outdo the other. The result was a rather eclectic amalgamation of foods and beverages. Luke's Mexican salsa, tamales and Chinese egg rolls. Cat's spaghetti and meatballs and Greek salad. Everyone was having a great old time.

With the exception of the host.

Cat was across the living room putting the finishing touches to the buffet with a huge leafy something in a red ceramic pot. She'd persuaded him to buy half a dozen plants at the store, insisting he lived a sterile existence without living things around him. No matter that Luke knew he'd never remember to water the things.

He remembered the alarming amount of plants scattered around his dad's house, but had given up without too much of a fuss. Cat was a born nurturer. She needed to be needed, even if by just a few houseplants.

He felt as nervous as a mother bird pushing her chick out of the nest for the first time. Luke watched her without seeming to, and tried to see her as his friends would. With his luck they'd have the immediate hots for her.

At the moment Cat was the center of attention of a pack of chest puffing, lip smacking, posturing males. Luke monitored the behavior of his friends with a jaundiced eye. They might as well let her inspect their teeth, check their brokerage statements and call old girlfriends for references.

Mike leaned close to whisper in Cat's ear. She

laughed. The sound rippled just beneath the music. Luke felt it in his gut.

Her looks were addictive, her compelling, innocent sensuality impossible to ignore. God knows, he was trying. Her sassy mouth and sharp wit were destined to drive some lucky guy to the brink of madness. His friends circled her like sharks in a feeding frenzy. He intercepted a lascivious look from Ted, so busy flexing his muscles and trying to hide his receding hairline he didn't even notice Luke's warning glower from across the room.

"If you keep glaring like that no one will go near her." Nick raised his voice to be heard over the music, and handed him a beer. "All they're doing is talking about the stock market."

Luke pulled the tab, then took a swig. "Allan had his hand on her ass." Cat wore perfectly respectable, not-too-tight, black pants and a teal T-shirt. She wasn't wearing jewelry, and hardly any makeup. And she outshone every woman there.

"And a very sweet ass it is, too," Nick said. "Chill. The whole point of this soirée is for Catherine to meet people. She's doing fine. Leave her alone."

"I need to stick close. She was really nervous about tonight."

"Nervous about what? Meeting our degenerate friends?"

Luke shrugged, covertly studying the dynamics of the group surrounding her. "I guess." The guys were salivating as they watched her eat an egg roll. "She didn't have much of a social life in Beaverton. I told her the city was too fast-paced for her."

"Ho, boy." Nick chuckled. "In other words, you challenged her."

Paul elbowed Mike out. Decent guy, Paul. A good eight inches shorter than Cat. No one held that squint against him.

Luke turned his glare on Nick. "Challenged her? I was trying to protect her."

Nick took a swig of his beer, eyeing his friend over the can. "By telling an intelligent, attractive woman she'd be out of her depth in the city?"

Across the room Cat did a quick sleight of hand, twisting and piling her hair on top of her head as she talked to Paul and the others by the open balcony door. All that hair around her shoulders must be hot. Still, he'd have to warn her how provocative the pose looked. As her T-shirt pulled across her moving breasts, Rob just about swallowed his tongue.

"She's not as self-confident as one might think," Luke muttered, not tasting the beer he chugged. Allan strolled up and formed another wall around Cat. He said something; she smiled, showing pretty white teeth and no desire to drop the hand she held provocatively on top of her head.

Nick smiled. "Doesn't look the least bit nervous to me."

An annoying tick started in Luke's right eyelid. He scowled. "She's biting her bottom lip. See? There," he muttered. "She did it again."

"God, yes," Nick enthused. "Very sexy."

"That's a sign she's nervous, you sex maniac." Luke glared at him, then narrowed his eyes when he saw the way his friend's eyes lit up with devilry. "What?"

"Huh?" Nick asked, all innocence.

"Whatever you're plotting, forget it. I don't want her hurt."

"Got it." Nick saluted. Without missing a beat, he asked mildly, "Sooo...what happened to Karen?"

"Karen?"

"The girlfriend du jour?"

"I know who Karen is. She's around here somewhere."

"Where's Catherine?"

"Over by the CD flirting with... You're looking at her, you lamebrain. Why're you asking me?"

"Don't you think it's a little odd that you don't know where your girlfriend is, but you know Catherine's exact location in a crowded room?"

"No," Luke said shortly. "I don't. It's my job to take care of her. Didn't you come with a date?"

"Are you kidding?" Nick grinned. "And have to look and not partake of this delectable smorgasbord of single women? You invite me to a feast, then expect me to bring a bag lunch?"

"I wanted to give Cat a reasonable selection. It would've looked a little obvious if I'd invited just guys. Not to mention boring."

"And I'm eternally grateful. You did good."

"Putting this together was a lot of hard work."

"Especially since Catherine was the one who did all the hard work," Nick said dryly. "A ten spot says Ted will be date number one."

Luke snorted. "He's showing her that stupid scar he got when he fell off my roof last summer. Probably spinning her some far-fetched tale."

"Women go for that stuff."

"Nah," Luke said absently. The tick over his eye was really getting on his nerves now. "It'll be Allan. Twenty, on..." He peered across the room. Ted had his hands on the back of Cat's neck. "What does he think he's doing? Excuse me a sec."

"It's just a casual massage." Nick snagged his arm. "Uh-uh. Better change that plan, old son. Incoming. Karen at three o'clock." His smile widened.

"Don't you have moves to make?" Luke muttered.

"You betcha. I'm off to give the guys some competition."

Luke swore under his breath as his friend threaded his way across the crowded room to Cat's side. She gave Nick a wide, friendly smile and took his offered hand. He led her to the small area where a few couples were dancing.

Nick was a suave, good-looking guy. Women liked Nick. Luke himself was a decent-looking guy, and just as suave as Nick was. Women liked him, too. Which was why they were going to protect Cat from smooth-talking men like themselves. That's what Nick had meant.

Competition? Luke watched them walk into each other's arms and move to the dreamy music. Slowly. Competition? Nick? What a repugnant thought.

Ridiculous.

Out of the question.

Luke dragged his focus away from Cat snuggled in Nick's arms to watch Karen shimmy closer. His date looked dazzling in a short, tight red dress, black hair streaming down her bare back, long legs showcased to perfection in red high heels. He didn't feel a single solitary spark. Nothing. Nada. Zip.

Obviously he was a sick man.

Karen slid her arm about his waist. Her perfume, recently applied, smelled great. Unfortunately, it didn't do a thing for him. She looked up at him with heavy-lidded, sultry brown eyes. "Hi, sweetie. Miss me?"

Luke bit back the truth. Karen was a nice woman. He'd invited her to the party. Now he couldn't wait to take her home. And leave her there. Alone.

"Sorry." He cupped her cheek and smiled ruefully. "I've practically ignored you all night, haven't I? It's been so long since I threw one of these things. I forgot how much work it is. Let me change the CD, and I'll give you my undivided attention." As soon as he could manage to unglue his twitching eyes from Cat and Nick, who were like Siamese twins on the postage-size dance floor. Luke took Karen's hand and led her to the state-of-the-art CD player, where he changed the selection of slow ballads to something loud, fast and energetic. His choice was met with a series of catcalls from his party guests. Tough.

He wrapped an arm around Karen's bare shoulders and led her to the middle of the dancers. She moved into his arms smoothly and, despite the pulsing beat of the music, rested her head against his chest and twined her arms about his waist. She moved sensuously against him.

The problem was, Luke thought, enfolding her in his arms, she was just too...short. That was it. She was too short. She didn't fit. Even wearing those heels, the top of her head only came to the middle of his chest. Which was really too bad. Karen was beautiful, smart, sexy. How unfortunate he'd never noticed how vertically challenged she was before tonight.

With fifty-plus bodies in it, the room was hot. Even with the door wide-open to the narrow balcony, the evening air was stifling. Luke wanted to unpeel Karen from his chest and stand under a cold shower. He concentrated on moving his feet.

Two yards away, Cat danced with Nick, laughing and chatting and having the time of her life. Luke would have to talk to her. He'd invited at least seven guys specifically for her to meet tonight. She already knew Nick.

Luke rubbed his hand down Karen's smooth arm and turned her so that his back was toward Cat and he could give his date the attention she deserved. Karen slid her hands up his chest and around his neck.

"Too many people here." She ran her long nails up and down the back of his neck. "Bet no one would notice if we snuck out."

LUKE SAT IN THE BACK ROW of the dark, all-night movie theater. He could have had his pick of greasy, red velvet seats. He was the only one there. Not surprising. It was 2:00 a.m. and an artsy foreign film flickered on the screen, the subtitles barely legible. At this very moment he should have been getting hot and sweaty with Karen. Instead he'd dropped her off, walked her to the door and driven back into the city.

He didn't want to go home, because he wanted to go home so badly he could taste it.

Nuts. He was certifiably nuts. He wasn't sure who he was doing this for. Cat or himself.

LUKE DIDN'T COME HOME.

He and his gorgeous, petite brunette with boobs out to there and legs up to here had disappeared over an hour ago. Catherine refused to speculate where they were or what they might be doing. Might? Ha! Did every woman he lusted after have to be so petite? So available? So...cute? She clenched her teeth.

Ducking out on his own party was rude as far as she was concerned. The condo was still jam-packed with Luke's and Nick's upwardly mobile friends, none of whom seemed to have noticed their host had gone AWOL. Everyone was having a blast.

Catherine's head throbbed and the muscles around her mouth ached from smiling. She was tired of making nice. In fact, she'd pretended to hurt her ankle so she didn't have to dance any more. Which meant she was stuck sitting in Luke's big black leather chair in the corner with her feet propped up. A captive audience for Ted, Allan, two Bobs and an ethereal blonde named Cheryl.

She let Cheryl entertain the four men while she zoned out, thinking unwillingly about what Luke was up to. Karen had beautiful skin. No freckles on her. Catherine glanced down at her own hands, fisted around a half-filled glass of warm soda. Her skin looked as though she'd been peppered. Ugh. She hated her freckles. Hated them.

One of the Bobs said something, and the others laughed. Catherine had enough presence of mind to smile. One thing she'd learned: there was no point in crying over things that couldn't be changed. She was in this particular polka-dotty skin, and she had to resign herself to living with it. Disliking how she looked wasn't going to change reality.

Besides, she thought, working herself up into a real snit, it was Luke's fault. If he hadn't always shown up with some creamy-skinned, pocket Venus, Catherine wouldn't have grown up hating her freckles, her hair and her height.

She wanted Luke to come home and everyone else to disappear.

Eventually, finally, the guests left in dribs and drabs. Now it was after two, and Luke still wasn't back.

The last to leave, Nick leaned over to kiss her forehead on the way out the front door. "Are you sure I can't—"

"Go." Catherine pushed at his wide chest. "Thank you for offering to help with the cleanup. I'll take care of it next week when I wake up."

"You did good, Princess. You were the belle of the ball."

"I'm delighted to hear it." Catherine didn't bother to stifle a yawn. "Too bad Prince Absent wasn't here to see me shine."

"Oh, he saw enough. Trust me."

"You're a sweet man. Delusional, but sweet. Go home, Nick."

As soon as the door closed behind him, Catherine felt the muscles in her shoulders sag. Overtired, that was all. She was just overtired. Overstimulated. Overloaded.

She imagined Luke in bed with Karen. The salsa and meatballs did a sickening dance in her tummy. She gathered several empty platters from the dining room table on her way to the kitchen for a Maalox.

After changing into plaid flannel pajama bottoms, one of Luke's T-shirts and her ratty slippers, she shuffled back into the living room and turned off the CD player. Ah. Silence.

She surveyed the messy room, knowing no matter how tired, she wouldn't be able to sleep. She almost had herself convinced it had nothing to do with Luke's absence and everything to do with not waking up to this mess.

"You owe me, Van Buren. You owe me big." She loaded dirty glasses onto a tray and wrinkled her nose. A sickening rush of memories assaulted her. She couldn't smell beer without remembering that night nine years ago.

It had started harmlessly enough; her friends, fake IDs in hand, had surprised her with a visit to a strip joint for her seventeenth birthday. Catherine didn't want to remember the rest of it. If she did, she'd be on the next plane back to Beaverton.

One thing was for certain—the next time she managed to get Luke to kiss her she'd make sure she was stone cold sober. That was then. This was now.

Same objective. Different game plan. She'd chosen this path, and she'd stick to it. No retreating like a spineless crab. Nothing ventured, nothing gained. Rah rah rah.

She looked down at her clothing and grimaced. Not exactly seductive. But if she suddenly appeared in a slinky black negligee and garter belt, Luke would run screaming for the hills. No. She had to take this slowly and methodically. She'd put the idea out there. Luke had to run with it.

She just had to have the courage of her convictions and not run when the going got tough.

It took more than an hour to clean up the party mess. Luke still wasn't home. "Of course he isn't. What did you expect?" she asked herself, drying the last platter and putting it away while the dishwasher hummed with the final load. "You aren't the only woman who wants him. Duh, Catherine!"

She had to play her cards close to her chest. This time Luke had to make the first move. She just had to be patient. One of her better traits, and one not shared by Luke.

She checked the living room and narrow balcony one last time for stray glasses. Finding none, she went to turn off the kitchen light before going to bed. The place was now spotless. Luke called her a neat freak. Okay, so she was a little obsessive. He was just the opposite. For a man meticulous in his work, Luke was a slob at home. He'd happily leave the same pair of dirty socks, breeding and multiplying, under the coffee table until they walked to the laundry on their own.

Her habits had been ingrained before the age of six. She and her mother had moved seven times, sometimes in the dead of night. If everything was in its place, she'd been able to grab her most precious possessions quickly.

She glanced at the clock on the stereo: 3:30 a.m.

They'd be asleep now. Cuddled together. Karen

probably had one of those froufrou beds, all lace and pink pillows. Luke would look outrageously masculine and sexy, stretched out naked—

Catherine ruthlessly cut off the thought and groaned out loud. Living with Luke was going to either kill or cure her.

5

LUKE SNEAKED INTO his own apartment like a thief in the night. He'd seen that foreign film so many times he swore he could now speak fluent German. He frowned. All the lights in the spotless living room were on. Unbuttoning his shirt, he pulled it free of his pants and felt a twinge of guilt for leaving Cat to do the cleanup. Then he considered how he'd have felt if he'd stuck around. Hell, he'd done the right thing.

He almost had a seizure when he saw Cat sprawled out on the leather sofa. She wore one of his favorite ratty T-shirts and a disreputable pair of pajama bottoms he swore she'd had since she was a kid. Her cheeks were pink; her eyes glittered.

"Nice of you to drop by, Van Buren. Pleasant evening?"

"Delightful," Luke managed to answer cheerfully. Man, was she ticked. He stuffed his hands into the pockets of his chinos as he walked around the arm of the sofa. "Hey, thanks for doing the cleanup. Did Nick give you a hand?"

"Yes. By leaving."

Cat drew a leopard print pillow, which hadn't been here a week ago, onto her lap, still glaring. Whoops. He did a quick scan through the open door into the darkened bedroom and lowered his voice. "Are we alone?"

Her cheeks lit up like flamingo-pink neon. "Other than the entire 49ers team naked, and exhausted, in the bedroom, you mean?"

Luke took his hands out of his pockets and sat on the opposite arm of the sofa. Out of missile reach. "It's not out of the realm of possibility that you'd have a man here, Cat."

Her fiery eyebrows shot up into her bangs. "Who are you? What alien life force took over Luke Van Buren's body?"

"Huh?"

"Whose condo is this? I hadn't met any of these people here tonight before in my life! Do you really think I'd sleep with a total stranger? In your home? In your bed?"

"Ahh, no."

"Then don't ask such asinine questions, you turkey."

She curled her legs under her and bunched up her hair in her fist. She wasn't wearing a bra. He remembered that brief, tantalizing flash of cinnamon and cream, and almost licked his lips. Yep, Luke thought. A good thing he'd stayed out.

"Shouldn't you be sleeping?" he asked mildly. What was the point in sitting in a movie theater all night only to came home and find her wide-awake, sexy as hell and in his face?

"I just finished shoveling everything into the dishwasher."

The hectic color had left her cheeks. Her eyes looked bruised and kind of sad, Luke thought. They would have been looking a damn sight sadder if he'd hung around much longer at the party.

"I would've cleaned up in the morning, Cat."

She hugged the pillow and snorted. "Yeah, right."

"So what did you think of Ted?"

She shrugged.

"Allan?"

She did the so-so thing with her head.

"Either of the Bobs? Any of them?"

Cat unfolded her legs. She was close enough to touch. The scent of her body, warm, female, Catherine, made him dizzy.

"Come on, Cat."

"Hey, don't rush me. I'll keep you posted. You've given me enough to work with for now." She stood looking down at him. "How'd your evening with Karen go?"

"Great." *The pits.* Karen had not been a happy woman when he'd left her at her door.

"She seems nice enough."

"Pretty, smart. She's a lawyer."

"Lovely," Cat told him coolly. "She can do your prenup if you two get married."

"She knows that'll never happen."

Luke rose. They were no more than a foot apart. Desperate to steal a kiss from those sweet pink lips, he knew she'd deck him with the pillow she clutched to her midriff.

"Ever heard of common law?"

"This is the second time I've dated her. Besides, Nick and I have The Bet, remember?"

Cat shook her head, slapping him in the face with

twenty pounds of hair. The honey-scented strands lashed his cheeks before springing back home. He wanted to grab her by that hair, wrestle her back to the sofa...and get a swift kick in the *cojónes* for his trouble.

"That is one of your more ridiculous bets, Luke. What if one of you falls madly in love and *wants* to get married before you're thirty-five? It could happen, you know."

"Being in love doesn't necessarily mean marriage. Which is why I consider The Bet a sure thing. I have the edge. I'm never getting married, however old I am."

"You mean you still believe that stupid 'all your emotional eggs in one basket' theory you had at fifteen? That, my darling dragon, is what we women call Lack of Commitment. You just haven't met the right woman yet."

"I meet the right women. Several times a year. Which has always been my point." He frowned. "Are you going to bed?"

"Yes." She stepped out of reach and turned to assess him over her shoulder. "Are we going to the house tomorrow?"

"Yeah. Late-ish. Take the bed again."

He watched her walk to the bedroom. Even in the too large T-shirt, she moved like music. Fluid, graceful and too sexy for his peace of mind. Luke closed his eyes. He needed something else to focus on when Cat was around. Something that wasn't soft, smooth and cinnamon flavored. Something like—

"Sweet dreams, Luke."

"Yeah, you too, honey." Something like—construction. Yeah. That was it. Instead of seeing Cat, he'd imagine building the house. From the foundation up.

"Are you okay?"

He glanced up. She was standing at the bedroom door with a little V of worry between her brows, one slippered foot perched on the other. He wanted to stride over, pick her up, carry her into the bedroom, lay her on his nice, wide bed...

"Just tired."

Excavating the foundation. Lots of dirt. Big piles of dark soil—soft pale, freckly mounds tipped with pale apricot nipples... "See you in the morning," he said gruffly, getting up to click off the light and plunge the room into darkness.

He heard the door shush closed.

Yeah, this visualizing concept stuff was going to work well. Yeah, right!

AN HOUR LATER, still wide-awake, with excavating the furthest thing from his mind, Luke had to go to the bathroom. To get to the bathroom, he had to go through the bedroom. He dreaded walking through the room with Cat sleeping there. Why had he decided to combine two bedrooms into one? Why had he thought a bigger kitchen warranted removing the guest bath?

Because he hadn't expected Cat to be sleeping in his bed. That's why.

She's sleeping, you moron, Luke told himself, tiptoeing into the bedroom. She'd left the light on in the bathroom. A sliver of golden light slashed across her figure on the bed.

"Ah, Cat," he said softly.

She was sprawled facedown across the bedspread, her hair covering her face and half the pillow. Out like a light. Beside her, tucked up to its furry little armpits by the blanket, was the teddy bear he'd given her years ago. That was Cat. She hung on to things. Treasured things. Coddled things.

He noticed she'd changed his satin sheets for plain white cotton. He sighed and bent to take off her slippers.

The smart thing to do, Catherine decided as she felt Luke's hands removing her left fuzzy slipper, was to turn over and say hi. The sensation of his warm hands on her bare foot sent little electrical currents up her leg.

Pretending to be asleep now was almost as bad as when she'd hidden under his bed on one of his weekends at home. She'd been about nine. Even then she'd wanted to be as close to him as she could get. Eventually he'd discovered her, and hadn't cared that she was faking a deep sleep. He'd hauled her out, dragged her screaming into the hallway, then slammed the door in her face.

The housekeeper had reported the incident to his father, who in turn had punished Luke, and in a natural progression, Luke had refused to talk to Catherine for a month.

Bad idea then. Bad idea now.

He drew off the other slipper, then massaged her instep with strong, sure strokes. She'd never felt anything more erotic in her life. Goose bumps broke out on her skin as he cradled her foot before gently settling it back on the bed.

She felt the drag of the covers under her as Luke carefully pulled the spread and blankets down to her feet, trying not to wake her. Her breasts tingled as if he'd touched them directly. She imagined the glide of the blankets were Luke's hands skimming slowly down her body. Eyes squeezed shut, she pictured his hands on her. Large, hard, long fingered. Smoothing, cupping, claiming.

Moisture pooled between her thighs. Her pulse pounded strategically. She gritted her teeth at the thick, syrupy pleasure her imagination created. She felt the brush of fur, and realized he'd settled Hubert back beside her cheek.

"You're a real pain, Catherine Anne Harris, you know that?" Luke murmured. "I wish you'd stayed in Oregon where you belong."

It took a moment for her overactive hormones to assimilate what he'd just said. *A real pain. Stayed where you belong.*

The delicious sensations left her body in a dizzying rush.

Her heart ached in her chest; the back of her nose tingled. She clamped her teeth together so tightly her jaw ached. So much for wanting Luke to make the first move. He didn't want her. Biblically or otherwise.

No matter how Luke presented his invitation for her to stay, the bottom line, as usual, was that she was in the way. All her life she'd been in the wrong place at the wrong time where Luke was concerned.

Catherine wanted to run. She wanted to go home. To her own bed, with her own safe things surrounding her. But she'd burned those bridges by selling the house and putting everything she owned into storage. At the time that had taken more courage than she'd thought she could muster. But selling and closing up the only real home she'd ever known had been child's play compared to this.

Luke tucked the covers around her, brushing aside her hair. For a brief, electrifying second, his hand lingered on her nape.

She couldn't help it. She shivered.

He swore under his breath.

For several seconds he didn't move. She could feel him standing there beside the bed. Looking at her. Then she heard his footsteps as he went into the bathroom. The lock snicked. The shower turned on.

Catherine stared up into the darkness, eyes dry, chest aching.

LUKE FINALLY EMERGED from a restless sleep. He hadn't bothered with a sheet. The leather sofa had glued itself to his skin all the way down his left side, and he had to peel himself off like a giant Band-Aid. Thoroughly out of sorts, he yanked last night's chinos over his briefs and staggered reluctantly through the bedroom to get to the bathroom.

The bed was neatly made. How nice. One of them had slept well. He glanced at the bathroom door. Open. He shot a look at his watch. Great. He'd had about three hours sleep. And where was Cat at eight on a Sunday morning?

After a quick, hot shower, he dressed in his favorite denim cutoffs and a faded red tank top, then headed for the kitchen.

Wherever she'd gone, Cat had unloaded the dishwasher and put everything neatly away before she'd left. He hadn't heard a sound. He searched around for a note. She hadn't left one. Vaguely miffed, he started coffee and decided on eggs Benedict for breakfast. He didn't just save his culinary masterpieces for The Morning After. Although he usually cooked this particular dish for two. And served it in bed.

AS SOON AS SHE WALKED into the kitchen, Catherine knew she should have stayed out longer. There was a twenty-four-hour movie theater two blocks away. She could have spent the morning there, reading subtitles.

"Good morning, sleepyhead," she said cheerfully, setting a bag of doughnuts and the Sunday paper on the counter to avoid looking at a lot of naked Luke. Tanned, taut, terrific body. Not a freckle in sight. He had the naturally long, lean physique of an athlete without having to do the maintenance. It wasn't fair. But then, what in life was? A familiar tightness gripped her chest.

She turned and reached up to find a mug in the overhead cabinet. "Fun party. I like your friends."

"The feeling was mutual." Luke eyed her black biker shorts and white tank top without comment. There were no secrets between fabric and skin, and despite having been outside jogging in the park, Catherine suddenly felt self-conscious in her skimpy attire. Luke's gaze traveled the length of her legs and back up again to her sweat-damp hair scraped back in a ponytail.

"Been running?"

"Yeah. Across the street in the park."

Even at 7:00 a.m. Marina Green had been crowded with bikers, runners, mothers with little kids, people on in-line skates. None of them had looked at her the way Luke was doing right now. None of them could make her shiver with a mere glance. She filled her mug with cool tap water, drank it down, then casually picked up the half-filled carafe of coffee and poured herself a cup.

Golden sunlight bathed Luke as he sat at the table in the alcove. His skin looked like bronze satin, a cliché, but true. Muscles he'd acquired from hard physical labor, not weights, covered his bones in a fascinating display of hills and valleys. There wasn't an ounce of fat on the man anywhere. And Catherine could pretty much see everywhere.

That faded red tank top didn't hide much. She tried not to stare at a flat brown nipple, showing because he'd twisted to watch her, and the wide armhole had shifted.

She found the milk and sugar and doctored her coffee, then grabbed the white paper bag off the counter.

"There's a gym on the ninth floor," he reminded her as she sat down opposite him at the table.

"Ah, yes. Where you go to pick up babes. I prefer being outside in the fresh air. Want a doughnut?"

Luke shook his head. She shivered as his hair brushed his neck. "I just had breakfast. I left yours in the oven." He looked her up and down. "You're in pretty good shape."

"Pretty good shape?" Catherine pushed aside the greasy bag and rose from the table to flex the biceps in

her right arm. "I'm in my prime, pal, and don't you forget it."

He snagged her wrist and held it up. "Look at this,
your bones are as delicate as a bird's. I could snap this
wrist with no trouble at all."

Catherine disengaged her hand. "If you snapped my
wrist you'd have trouble, all right. You'd be wearing
the coffeepot around your neck." Goose bumps shot
up her arm.

"See, that's what I mean. You look fragile enough to
break in a man's hands, but you have an amazing resil-
ience—" He broke off and gave her a look she couldn't
hope to interpret.

"Mix fragility with all that firehouse red hair, and a
man would have to be deaf, dumb and blind not to
want the whole package in his be—life. You're a lethal
combo, Cat. They're going to kill themselves falling
over their feet, and each other, to have you. And I'm
here to make sure the right guy gets the prize. I'm going to keep you by my side, and protect you from the
predators, until you make your choice."

It was fascinating to hear his assessment of her. He'd
rarely commented on her appearance over the years.
She knew his preferences from seeing the women he
dated. Petite blondes or brunettes. Not gangly, freckly
redheads. So it felt odd to have Luke's entire attention
focused on her. Especially at such close quarters.

"I don't need you to protect me, Luke. Although I
appreciate the offer. The thought of half a dozen guys
trying to coerce me into bed is incredibly appealing."
She grinned at him. "I'd like the chance to fight off a
few of them myself." She forced herself not to rub her

wrist, where his touch seemed to have burned her skin like a brand.

Luke gave her a quirky look. "Am I going to have to impose a curfew?"

"You could try." Catherine smiled sweetly. "Although I believe people are capable of having sex at any time of day or night, aren't they?"

"They, maybe. You, no. You aren't the type to fall into bed with a sweet talking man."

"I'm not? Then why did you ask me who I was sleeping with after the party?"

He scowled. "I had to ask. Didn't mean I thought... Cat, you've waited twenty-six years to shed your virginity. I know you. You'd have to be madly in love with the guy. That takes time. Years."

"Years?"

"Hell, yes. Years." Luke drained his mug and set it carefully on the table. He gave her a serious, now-listen-to-me-kid look. "You want more than animal coupling. More than lust. You want love, respect, understanding. Someone who knows you, who'll allow you to fulfill your potential as a woman." He looked so serious she had to smile.

"Can't I go for a little animal coupling first?"

"Catherine."

"Maybe you and Nick have the right idea. Maybe I should be like you guys for a while before I settle down."

"Like...us? You mean be a...player?" His voice rose. "A lifestyle that's risky, shallow, empty? A nowhere existence, just living for the moment?"

"Sure. Why not? It works for you. I'll play the field, be a party girl. That's a great idea, Luke."

He scowled at the implication that it had been his idea. "You're a woman."

"There are women players. You date them."

"And you're about as far from a player as—as Bambi is from Caligula." The light went on. "Aha! You're just trying to muddy the issue."

"I just thought while I look, I might enjoy living on the edge. Wild, uninhibited, unrepentant sex. Variety—"

"Over my dead body."

"Sheesh, that's a little drastic. I might as well wear a chastity belt." Thank God he looked so appalled. She had no idea what she would've said next. She put up her hand. "Just kidding. Can we change the subject now, please?" Catherine rose from the table and yanked open the oven door. "You mentioned real food?"

"You throw something like indiscriminate sex into the conversation and then want to eat?"

"Sure. We changed the subject. Oh, yum. Eggs Benedict."

She took the plate from the oven, feeling his gaze on her backside. That bit of conversation had thrown them both. She repressed a smile as she uncovered the plate he'd saved for her.

Catherine was amazed that the things Luke cooked turned out so well. He never measured anything, adding and subtracting ingredients to suit his taste buds, which just showed how different the two of them were.

She stuck religiously to the recipe, lined up the ingredients and utensils in the order they'd be used, and never varied anything by so much as half a grain of salt. If she had a kitchen it would consist of natural woods and a jungle of green plants. With a place for everything, and everything in its place.

The condo kitchen was a gourmet chef's dream, with brushed-chrome doors, wide black-marble countertops and a ceiling rack laden with gleaming, well-used copper pots. The counters were cluttered with weeks' worth of newspapers, fancy coffeemakers, a Cuisinart, all sorts of high-tech gadgetry, five pairs of sunglasses and a lonely sock.

In the deep windowsill, Luke had his only concession to plants. The window box Catherine had planted for him when he'd first moved in still flourished. She'd crowded it with various herbs he snipped for cooking. An automatic drip system hooked to the faucet guaranteed the plants' lives.

"Delish," Catherine told him, after swallowing. "Oh. I passed Nick in the lobby. He has a present for you."

Luke set down his coffee mug. "Why?"

"Not what?"

"I know Nick. He's a sneaky devil. If I know the why, I can guess the what."

"You won't guess what this is, I promise."

"Hmm." Luke's glassy focus was in the vicinity of her chest. He must have zoned out, thinking about something, but it still felt as though he were looking. Her nipples peaked to full glory. She casually crossed her arms and leaned forward to brace them against the edge of the table, just in case he wasn't as zoned out as she feared. "Luke?"

His head shot up. This wasn't their usual comfortable conversation. It felt a little strained, she thought, but that was her problem. Luke didn't know she'd heard him last night in the bedroom. Remembering his comments sent a chill skittering through her like dead leaves on frozen ground. Was he trying to find a compassionate way to tell her he wanted her to leave? He'd done it before with devastating effect.

"Oh, yeah. Sorry. I was thinking about—about the foundations for the house."

Catherine looked at him blankly. "There's something wrong with the foundation and you only realized this now?"

"Nope. Nothing wrong. Solid. Firm. Perfect." He picked up his empty mug and brought it to his mouth.

"I think you'd better start taking vitamins." She snatched his mug out of his hand and refilled it. "Here. I'm off to grab a shower." She loaded her plate and cutlery into the dishwasher and avoided Luke's eyes, miserable coward that she was.

"And then I'm going to pack." Catherine nudged the door closed with her knee and resolutely turned to face him.

"Pack?" he asked blankly.

"Pack." She infused as much chirpy good cheer as she could muster into the words. "Let's face it. This wasn't one of my better ideas, Luke. I'm going home." *Before I make a fool of myself and you tell me to go.*

"Running, Cat?"

"That's not fair."

"What about finding a husband?"

"I can do that in Beaverton."

"You should've thought of that before you sold the only home you've ever known. Where will you live, little sister?"

Her chest ached. "I'll buy a condo, big brother."

"Sounds like a giant hassle to me." His knuckles whitened around his mug. "Besides, we decided you'd stay here. Why buy another condo when in a few weeks this one will be available? Consider it a favor, Cat. I can stay with you when I work late."

"I'm sure my husband will be thrilled to have you tromping through our bedroom to use the bathroom," she said dryly.

"You don't have a husband." He gave her a penetrating look. "It's not like you to make impulsive decisions like this, Cat. What's going on?"

"It's my prerogative to change my mind."

"Not when we have a bet going, it isn't."

"Oh, for heaven's sake! You and your dumb bets! Who cares?"

His chair screeched across the glossy, black-vinyl floor as he shoved it back. "*I* care. It's a matter of honor."

Catherine rolled her eyes. "Give me a break, Van Buren. I admit I made a monumental mistake coming to you. I don't fit in here. I don't blend in with your yuppie friends." She spread her arms. "Look at me—"

Luke squeezed his eyes shut as if he were in pain. "Go take a shower. We'll discuss this when you're dressed."

"SHE WANTS TO GO back home," Luke hissed, eyes fixed on the slammed-shut bedroom door. He stuck his bare feet up on the coffee table and glared at his friend. "What happened last night at the party?"

"Other than the host being eighty-sixed?" Nick asked as he reached for another doughnut.

"I had to take Karen home."

"And Catherine got in a snit when you were gone all night from your own party." Nick shook his head. "Women. Go figure."

"So? My entire social and sex life has to come to a screaming halt because Cat's here?"

Nick put up a powdered-sugar-coated hand. "Hey, that's your choice. Personally I wouldn't want to see anyone else. Not with Catherine around. In case you hadn't noticed, old son, that's one hot babe you have sharing your— Oh, excuse me," he drawled as Luke cleared his throat pointedly.

"I'd switch places with you in a heartbeat, and so would half our friends. Didn't you see them salivating around Catherine last night? Or were you too busy getting it on with Karen?"

"She's a beautiful woman."

"Cat? I know. She's gorgeous."

"Not Cat. Karen. And of course those degenerates were all over Cat like bears over honey. They're idiots, not stupid."

"What idiots aren't stupid?" Cat asked, emerging from the bedroom wearing white shorts, a black crop top and strappy black sandals. She'd even put on makeup. Nothing overt, just enough to make her look...*more*. She'd done something to tame her hair, then swooped it on top of her head in a sexy tumble held up by gravity. A forties pinup. Nick shot up from his seat and crossed the room in three strides.

"Let me take you away from all this, my lovely Princess Catarina." He grabbed Cat around her waist, touching her bare skin as he swirled her in a circle.

Luke watched through narrowed eyes, wondering where he could hide Nick's body after the homicide. His friend brought Cat's hand to his mouth, then theatrically kissed her fingertips before nibbling his way up her arm, reeling her in against his chest and making her laugh. Cat wrapped her arm around his waist and Nick smiled down at her.

"I brought you a present."

"I thought it was for me," Luke said, as a laughing Nick pulled Cat over to the new gate-legged table by the front door.

"Nope. You get yours later, old son. This one's for Catherine.

"Oh, Nick! Thank you." She picked up the old-fashioned, round fishbowl in both hands, then looked at Nick with shining eyes. There was only one ordinary little goldfish in the bowl, not an entire freshwater aquarium, Luke thought sourly as he watched them.

"This is so sweet of you."

"Hey, I'm a sweet guy—"

"You'd better change into jeans," Luke informed her, cutting Nick off. Preferably at the knees. "We're going on the bike."

"I'm not going on the bike. Allan's taking me."

Luke gave her a blank look. "To my house?"

"Is that a problem?" One hip cocked, she leaned

into Nick, holding the bowl with the lonely little fish against her chest.

Lucky fish.

"The sooner the house is finished the sooner you move in, right? Allan's a great painter. He told me so last night. Consider him free labor."

The two of them strolled across the living room like frigging Siamese twins. Nick dug in his pocket. Luke absently took the twenty his ex-best friend handed over as he passed.

"Yeah, I guess." He stuffed the money into his front pocket.

Cat didn't sound as if she were packing her bags anytime soon. Something inside him unwound a little.

"I'll make some calls and round up more people," he said. "We can make a day of it."

Cat glanced at her watch. "Well, an afternoon, anyway. You bet on Allan, did you?" she asked, then glanced at Nick. "Who was your call?"

"Ted."

"You should have told me. They both asked me out today."

"That would be cheating," Luke informed her, not amused that she was amused.

"Oh. Excuse me. I didn't realize there were rules." The doorbell rang and she disengaged from Nick. "That's Allan. Get the lead out, Van Buren."

She handed him the dumb fishbowl and went to the door.

6

NICK HAD GIVEN HIM a two-by-four. To beat back the guys who were going to swarm over Cat. No kidding. At the rate things were going Luke was going to need it. He didn't like the ratio of men to woman: three to one. In Cat's favor.

He liked women, and considered flirting one of life's greatest pleasures. But it was one of his unwritten laws that he never strung them along. Luke made no secret of his opinion of marriage or any long term commitment.

The second Cat had left on the arm of good old Allan, Luke called a woman he hadn't seen in months. Suzette was an attractive, petite brunette. Intelligent and witty, she made no bones about being available and she liked his rules just fine.

Half the twenty or so people spread throughout the house were working. The others had taken the grill across the street to the beach for an impromptu barbecue. Luke had posted a work schedule, and despite the moaning and groaning from his press-ganged crew, work was actually being accomplished.

Cat and Allan were painting the guest bedroom. They'd been in there for hours with the door closed. Of course, Luke thought, digging in one of the coolers for a liter bottle of soda, there was no furniture in there yet. But how long could it possibly take two people to paint a small room?

"Trying to use telekinesis to open the door?" Nick strolled into the kitchen and caught him glowering down the hall. Nick levered himself up onto the counter. "I thought you came in here for sodas."

"On my way." Luke held up the bottle and a short tower of paper cups. "Ladies getting twitchy?"

"Suzette and Kirsten wonder why everyone else is slaving serflike while you wander from room to room bossing us around."

"Meticulous planning." Luke shot another look toward the closed door down the hallway. "Bad idea leaving the two women unsupervised, Stratton. Who knows what devious plot they'll hatch while we're not paying attention? Back to work."

Nick slid off the plywood-topped counter. "Has Catherine said anything about leaving since we got here?"

"Nope."

"She and Allan look good together. What'ya think?"

It had been Luke's ridiculous reaction to Cat dragging Allan along that had induced him to invite five million people here in the first place. The house was overrun with bodies. Feeling incredibly beleaguered, he had to be in seven places at once to oversee what everyone was doing. "I think Allan's been in there with her long enough to paint the Sistine Chapel."

"Yeah? Go in there and supervise, then."

Luke swore. "Here, take these in to the ladies, I'll be right back." He handed Nick the soda and cups, then stalked out of the kitchen and down the hall.

Sitting cross-legged on the floor, Catherine glanced over her shoulder as the bedroom door flew open. Luke. She groaned dramatically and rolled her eyes, making Allan smile.

"He's *back!* Quick, look busy before he gives us another project."

"Har-dee har-har." In one glance, Luke assessed the freshly painted walls and half-painted trim. "Looks good. Nice job," he told Allan, then said to Catherine, "Can we talk a minute?"

She put her paintbrush down on the edge of the paint pan, then flexed her fingers as she rose. "Anything, as long as I can rest my poor abused arm."

Naturally, Luke was immaculately dressed, while she was covered from head to toe in cream-colored paint. Pounding music, the buzz of a Skil saw and manic hammering assaulted them from every direction as they walked through the house.

"What's up?" she yelled, following him out onto the front porch. Luke made a walking motion with his fingers and led her down the steps and across the scraggly front yard, then crossed the narrow street to the beach. The noise from the house dimmed, overshadowed by the whisper of waves curling up the beach. The gorgeous day was made absolutely perfect because she was with Luke.

Catherine removed her sandals and inhaled the salty air deep into her lungs. "Glorious. Beats paint fumes."

Several cheap laborers off to the right pretended to hide behind the sea grasses when they saw Luke coming down to the water. "Isn't lunch over?" he yelled.

"We haven't even lit the barbecue, Captain Bligh!"

Several of the men called out rude comments, which Luke volleyed back with laughing ease. People naturally gravitated to him. It was one of the things Catherine loved about him—that easy, relaxed warmth he exuded without even trying. He was such an extrovert, so charismatic that he made people happy to be near him. People always seemed to want to do their best when Luke was around.

Together they walked down the beach in the opposite direction of the rowdy lunch crew.

"You're lucky to have such great friends."

"Yeah. A good bunch. You fit in nicely. All the guys think you're hot. The women like you, too."

Catherine felt a warm glow. In the years she'd been taking care of their dad, she'd lost contact with many of her friends. She'd almost feared she might have lost some of her social skills. More than the words, the approval she heard in Luke's voice put a lump in her throat. She was glad she'd put off leaving for another day. She'd have one more Luke memory.

"Where are we going?" She skipped to keep up with his long strides. "Not, mind you, that I object to a break from slaving over a dripping paintbrush for a while."

"Let's sit over there in the shade." Luke pointed at a small sandy dune shaded by a wisp of a tree and tall sea grass. He leaned against the frail, gnarled tree trunk and stared out at the flat blue horizon for a few seconds without saying anything. Catherine's stomach clenched.

She concealed the frisson of unease that coursed through her, the sensation familiar and annoying. Old history. She usually managed to control it, but it still blindsided her every now and then. She'd felt it when her mother had left her with Peter Van Buren. She'd felt it every time Luke had tormented her as a child, insisting she was no relative of his. She'd felt it most profoundly the night of her seventeenth birthday, when Luke had rejected her amateurish advances. And she'd last felt it when the man she considered her father had died, eight months ago.

She didn't need a psychiatrist to tell her she had a fear of abandonment. *Don't be ridiculous,* she told herself, *no one is abandoning anyone.* Luke was everything he'd always been. A typical big brother. It wasn't his fault her feelings had grown and changed. And it would be unfair to blame him because his hadn't. Luke would never hurt her. At least not intentionally. Pulling her shell around herself like a crab and wanting to hide was a knee-jerk reaction. *Get over it,* she told herself firmly. She'd already decided to leave.

"If this is going to be a lecture about something, save your breath." Catherine sat gingerly on the hot sand and circled her bare knees with her arms. Wriggling her toes, she buried them in the dry, hot granules. "I'll be out of your hair tomorrow."

"That's what I wanted to talk to you about. Look, it's not like you have to go, is it? The house is sold. You said yourself you wanted to make a fresh start. The Bay area's great. In a month or so I'll be living out here, then you can finish turning the condo into the Amazon. Why leave now?"

She scratched a flake of cream paint off her shin. "I'm in the way."

"No you're not, Cat." Luke dropped to his knees beside her. He took her chin in his palm and made her look at him. "You're not in the way at all. I like having you with me."

His touch burned like a brand. Catherine shifted enough to dislodge his hand from her face. Her emotions were already on overload. All the old fears and doubts about making him see her differently came rushing to the fore.

The sun turned the short hairs on his arms the color of coffee; his skin shone with vitality. He was close enough for her to feel the brush of his shorts against her bare thigh. Close enough for Catherine to inhale his unique scent.

She loved him so much it hurt.

"It's a one-bedroom, Luke. And I'm in it. You can't even go to the bathroom without tripping over my stuff."

"I don't trip over your stuff. In fact, if I hadn't insisted you unpack, you'd still be living out of your suitcase. You're so neat I hardly notice you're there."

"You can't bring anyone home."

"At the moment I don't want to. And in the unlikely event that changes, I'll handle it. I'm not a sex fiend, Cat. As much as I'd like to tell you I have a smorgasbord of women who sleep over, I don't. Not nowadays."

"What about Suzette. Or Elizabeth the Wretch?"

"Both charming and delightful, but nothing serious."

"Yeah?"

"Yeah. Stay, Cat." He slung a brotherly arm around her shoulders. "Honest to God, I enjoy having someone to cook for. Besides, look how pink my nail beds are." He stuck a broad hand in front of her.

Catherine's lips twitched. "Your nail beds?"

"All that oxygen your rain forest is producing is good for me. And what would I do if I had the use of all my saucers again, or if I couldn't see the carpet because you weren't there to pick up my socks?'"

"You could get a maid, Van Buren."

The temptation to lean into him was overwhelming. His skin felt hot, and the sensation of having it touching hers zipped through her like expensive French champagne.

"A maid wouldn't keep me centered, or laugh at my jokes."

"Just promise me something, okay? If it starts getting to you, just come straight out and tell me. No hurt feelings."

"Never happen. You'll always have a home with me. Always."

She rested her head against his shoulder, hoping he couldn't see her moist eyes. "I love you, Luke Van Buren, do you know that?"

"I love you, too, Catwoman. A guy couldn't ask for a better baby sister."

Zing. Direct hit. After a stunned second, Catherine pressed her fingertips into her eye sockets. Hard.

Luke shifted beside her. "Are you okay?"

"Sand," she mumbled into her wrists. "Darn, that stings."

Not her eyes. Her heart.

"Want me to look?"

No, he wouldn't be able to see anything. He didn't

have twenty-twenty vision where she was concerned. "I'll be fine in a moment."

Give or take fifty years.

LUKE RETURNED to the house alone. Cat had decided to go for a run on the beach. He shook his head. The woman was insane. It was hot out there. He found Nick in the kitchen.

"Everything okay?"

"Yeah. Just had a little chat with Cat. She's staying."

"I'd have made book on that."

"Let's get some work done, Stratton." He and Nick crossed the entry hall side by side, their workboots vibrating on the subflooring. The front door stood open to catch the summer breeze, bringing with it the scent of briny air and the mouthwatering aroma of the beach barbecue. A couple of guys were out on the wide porch sanding, and the sweet smell of the sawdust mingled with the scents of tung oil, paint, and wallpaper paste.

Two different radios blared from opposite ends of the house, each on a different station, naturally—salsa from the back, hard rock from the front porch. Luke inhaled deeply as he stepped through the wide double doors into the great room. Home. It was becoming home.

Suzette and Kirsten, Nick's date du jour, a statuesque blonde of awesome proportions, glanced up as they strolled in, but the music was too loud to have a conversation, and they went back to staining the baseboards.

Nick poured more soda for the two women, then leaned back against the hearth to chug down his own drink before hunkering down to do a little hammering on the floor.

The stone fireplace soared to the cathedral ceiling. Dusty sunshine shone through the plastic-covered windows onto the oak plank floor. The plastic billowed with the breeze like an animal breathing.

Luke envisioned the room filled with his furniture. Two black leather sofas framing the fireplace. The steel wall unit over there. The metal sculpture there. His slick, stylized, monochromatic paintings grouped on the far wall.

He frowned.

Suddenly, a jungle of plants materialized next to the windows and animal print cushions on the sofas. A bowl with a single goldfish appeared on the steel-and-glass coffee table placed between the sofas.

Suzette rose from her position on the floor and sauntered over to give Luke a hug. "I hope that fearsome scowl isn't aimed at me." She raised her voice and ran a finger between his brows. She had straight white teeth and a very pretty smile. She smelled of Obsession. She had a brain.

She bored him to tears.

"Kirsten and I are declaring mutiny for a couple of hours so we can eat, then go for a swim. We'll come back in time to help you finish the floor in here, okay?" Suzette whipped her shirt over her head, exposing nicely tanned breasts and a flat midriff showcased in a minuscule white bikini. Luke's eyelids didn't even flicker. "Are you coming?"

He'd noticed the woman was barely dressed, but

didn't care. He pressed his fingertips into his temples and dredged up a smile. "Yeah. In a while."

Coming? It was a dim memory....

"YOU DON'T HAVE TO SKULK. I'm awake."

Luke looked adorably rumpled as he emerged from his cocoon of blankets to sit up the second she opened the front door the next evening. He'd left a lamp on for her, and the dimly shaded bulb cast a golden glow on his bare chest. He lay back against the arm of the sofa and eyed her yellow silk dress with approval. "You look very daffodilish. How'd it go with Ted?"

Catherine shrugged. "He knows a lot about fungus."

"He's a botanist."

She set her purse on the end table and took off her shoes. "I might never eat a mushroom again."

"Limiting, but not impossible. Will you see him again?"

Catherine shook her head, then picked up her shoes. "No sparks. Let me put it this way. You offered me white bread when what I crave is devil's food cake."

LUKE SAT ON NICK'S patio, a beer can balanced on his stomach, his bare feet crossed and propped up on the wrought-iron railing. It had been a swelteringly hot day, so they'd ordered pizza and taken a cold one outside. Now soft, damp fog misted around them as they sat in the dark and watched the lights across the Bay twinkle. Appear. Disappear. The fog oddly amplified, then dampened audio and visual details, making the foghorn sound close enough to touch tonight.

"Hey," Nick said lazily. "Guess who called today?

Rochelle Lemmon. She wants us to design the addition, after all."

Luke glanced at his partner. "Our way?" The Lemmon's Queen Anne Victorian was a magnificent lady. He and Nick had refused the commission the month before because the couple had insisted on modernizing the extension they wanted on the back of the house. Remodeling Victorians was not only Luke and Nick's specialty as architects, it was their passion.

"Balconies, stained glass, roof finials and all," Nick told him triumphantly, taking a swig of his beer. "I gave it to Christy to schedule."

Luke's mind raced ahead. He wanted their best craftspeople on this important job. There weren't that many artisans capable of doing the detailed and intricate work required. The characteristic excesses of the style—projected bay windows, towers, turrets, porches, wall carvings and acres of decorative trim and elaborate brackets—required a sure hand and a keen eye for detail.

"Willie to craft the chimneys. Mike McGuire for the crestings." Luke glanced casually at his watch. "If those two aren't done on the Simpson job, the Lemmons will just have to wait."

"They'll wait," Nick said with confidence. He and Luke had a sterling reputation, and their clients were prepared to wait. "Got a late date or something?"

"Cat's late. Monday was Ted. Tuesday night she went to a Giants game with one of the Bobs. On Wednesday, Allan took her over to Ghiradelli Square. Tonight she's at the symphony with Kevin. I've stopped asking who's next."

"That's the whole point, right? Meeting guys?" Nick shifted on his cushion. "What's the deal? Are you p.o.'d because she's a big hit and can change her dates twice as often as her underwear?"

"Do me a favor." Luke paused with the rim of the can poised below his mouth. He lowered the cold metal to his bare chest. "Don't mention Cat and underwear in the same breath, okay?"

He looked out at the faint phosphorescent line of the waves breaking on the beach beyond the wide swath of the park across the street. Several people were out walking their dogs despite it being eleven at night. He wondered what Cat and Kev were doing right now. The show would be over. Coffee, he guessed. Hopefully in a crowded place.

"You know, old son, sometimes you sound more like a jealous lover than a concerned big brother. Why is that, I wonder?"

"You should write fiction, Stratton. I'm merely concerned that Cat makes the right choices."

Luke felt as though he was going to jump right out of his too-tight skin. He wished to hell he could confide in Nick. He and Nick shared damn near everything. Not only did they own a business together, they were closer than most brothers. There was no one on this planet Luke respected and trusted more.

But Nick wasn't the problem. Luke was.

This was one secret he'd take to his grave. The second his feelings for Cat broke free from their tightly sealed box, he'd be in a world of hurt. Once out, he knew he'd never be able to shove those explosive emotions back where they'd been forced to lie dormant for years.

"And have you seen my place lately?" he said, desperate to change the subject. Which seemed to go from Cat to Cat without missing a beat. "It's overrun with foliage. If she buys one more plant I'll need a machete to get in the front door."

"She's nesting." Light glinted off the can as Nick lifted his beer to his lips by radar. "Look at all the antiques she's suddenly acquired. Shoot, in three weeks she's transformed the place. Plants, furniture, all those pillows, candles. Girl things. Hell, old son, if I didn't know better... Nah. Nothing. Neither of us has ever shacked up with a woman. So how would I know what it all means?

"Oh, by the way," Nick added lazily, "In case I didn't mention it before, Catherine's going out with me next week."

"You?" Luke heard a strange noise, then realized it was his teeth grinding. "'By the way?' Since when have you and Cat had that sort of relationship?"

"Hmm. Relationship." Nick's voice came out of the misty darkness like *The Phantom of the Opera.* "I kinda like the sound of that."

"Oh, no, you don't." Luke dropped his feet from the railing to the floor with a thump. "You keep away from Cat. She's not sophisticated like the women we date. She doesn't know how the games are played. She might fall for all your baloney, and you'll break her heart."

"I won't play with Catherine's heart. Trust me."

"I don't. Trust you, that is. And would you stop calling her 'Catherine' like that?"

"Like what? Her name is Catherine."

Luke's jaw hurt. "You'd better treat her as you've always done. Like a sister." His voice sounded like gravel in the thick darkness. He didn't wait for Nick to remind him that neither of them was Cat's brother. "She trusts you. Behave accordingly."

Their silence was punctuated by a mournful toot of the foghorn. A dog barked. A car shifted gears as it turned the corner. Ted and Cat? Impossible to see from this high up.

"How come you haven't taken her out?" Nick asked lazily.

"Me? I take her out all the time."

"I don't mean to your house to slave, you jerk. I mean on a date."

Luke crushed the can he held, then tossed it in the general direction of the pizza box on the floor. "That would be...not a good idea."

OVER THE NEXT COUPLE of days Luke couldn't stop thinking about Nick's question. Why couldn't he ask her out? They lived together. They were friends. Nothing wrong with asking a friend to the movies or a ball game, was there?

Offhand, he could think of several very good reasons why it would be a bad idea.

The promise to his dad.

The promise to Cat.

The promise to himself.

His—thus far contained—all-consuming lust.

On an "official date" he'd feel as though there was a chance of having more. And the reality was that this was Cat's time to shine. To get what she wanted. To get what she deserved.

She'd spent years cloistered in that big old house taking care of his father. Without complaint, without a murmur as life passed her by. She deserved every good thing there was.

A promise was a promise. It wasn't in him to renege, and he'd rather jump off a cliff than hurt her. Yeah, Luke decided, feeling sanctimonious, the least he could do was keep a low profile, and give Cat what she wanted.

VAN BUREN AND STRATTON owned an immaculately re-stored 1860s Italianate Victorian on the Avenues. It not only housed their flourishing business, it was a shining example of their talent as architects and restoration specialists. Every inch had been lovingly restored, then intricately painted.

There were memories for Catherine in every room of this house. There was a photograph of the three of them in Luke's office the day they'd opened their doors for business. She was proud that it was thanks to her skills as a day trader that Nick and Luke had been able to afford the house when they'd gone into business five years ago. She'd just begun day trading, and despite her show of confidence, wasn't sure at all whether she could make it in that volatile roller coaster world. But she'd flourished. By trading with the trends, she'd made steady profits, never making a huge killing but never getting wiped out, either, like other traders she knew.

She and Nick sat in the beautifully appointed reception area, which had originally been the ladies' parlor. She'd gone with Luke to buy the faded Aubusson area rug. She'd been with Nick when he'd found the camelback sofa in an out-of-the-way antique store.

"What I want," Catherine told Nick, "is for Luke to give some indication he sees me as more than someone making his socks magically disappear."

"Unless my friend has cataracts, I can't see how he can miss the obvious," Nick assured her, head down as he searched for something in the receptionist's antique cherry-wood desk.

Catherine had decided to drop in on Luke to see if he'd take her to lunch before she went shopping. He'd been out. But Nick had assured her he wouldn't be long.

A perfect opportunity for a little strategizing.

Nick dumped a pile of file folders on Christy's desk. Catherine winced. "What are you looking for?"

"The Stockton bids."

"It's in the file room in the blue file cabinet."

Nick glanced up. "It is? How'd you know that?"

"Because all bids go in the file room in the blue file cabinet. Nick? Could you stop scrounging around for a sec?"

Catherine tucked one foot under her and eased back on the stiff horsehair sofa, spread her soft skirt over her knees and picked up the cup and saucer from the table beside her. She'd acquired a slight tan at the beach a couple of days before, and the scoop-necked, butter-colored linen dress showed it off to advantage. The linen jacket hung neatly over a nearby tapestry chair. She cradled the saucer.

"In the last three weeks Luke's interrogated every single guy I've gone out with as if he's Don Corleone," she told Nick, exasperated. "He's still acting like my brother. I want him to see me as a sexy, desirable female, not his kid sister. I don't know how to make him see me as an adult woman."

"You look all-woman to me, Catherine. Trust me," Nick said dryly. "There wasn't a guy at the party who didn't sit up and take notice."

Catherine shot a wary glance at the etched glass panels in the oak front door before turning back to Nick. "I don't care about other men, Nick. I want Luke to love me."

Nick gave her a searching look, then said softly and with regret, "Will that really be enough for you, Catherine? Having him return your love? Luke's a great guy, but we both know he's got some serious hang-ups about commitment. Those fixed ideas he has about tying up his emotions too tightly. Can you accept that he'll never marry you?"

"Having him reciprocate what I feel will be enough."

"For how long?"

She looked him dead in the eye. "For as long as it lasts."

"Really?" Nick asked skeptically. "Then why did you ask him to find you a husband?"

"To throw him off the scent. Don't look at me like that. It's a given that marrying Luke would be a dream come true. But I know that will never happen. I know him, remember? I'm a lot more realistic than you give me credit for."

"Why do you love him, Catherine?" Nick asked. "Because you've know him almost your whole life? Because he represents security to you? Because you're alone now that your dad's gone?"

"No...maybe. Possibly that's part of it. A small part," she added quickly. "I love Luke because he's honest, and strong and ethical. Because he's got a sense of humor I understand. I love him because when I'm with him I'm...a better me. Does that make sense?"

"Yeah," Nick said with a smile. "It makes perfect sense. Okay, gorgeous, you have a master tactician at your disposal." He grinned, looking charmingly rakish. "Between us, he doesn't stand a chance."

"I want him, but not at the risk of destroying what we have now. You understand that, don't you?"

"Luke's right." Nick smiled. "You are a little crab. You've got to keep advancing here, Catherine. No retreating allowed."

"You're sure, positive, no doubt about it, I have a chance?" Catherine hated her own insecurity. She fought it every day, but sometimes that feeling of abandonment would creep up on her unexpectedly and she'd find herself poised for flight. "If you're sure I'm not making a total fool of myself..."

Nick came to sit next to her on the sofa and took both her cold hands between his. "You want Luke to see you as a woman, right? Then you have to make him stop seeing you as The Kid."

Like she hadn't been trying for the last decade. "And how do I go about doing that?"

Nick's blue eyes lit up devilishly as he released one hand to brush her mouth with his finger. "You dare Luke to teach you the art of seduction."

Catherine, in the process of lifting the delicate china cup to her mouth, almost choked. Her eyes went wide. "You're kidding, right?"

"Nope. Luke knows you don't have vast experience. Ask him to teach you."

Catherine carefully set the cup and saucer on the small fern table beside the sofa. "No one is that naive!"

"Luke thinks you are. Pretend, if you have to."

"I'm a lousy actress, Nick. Jeez-Louise, I'm not even a good poker player. How am I supposed to pull this off?"

"You'll figure it out." Nick, still holding her hand, looked up as the door opened and Luke walked in.

"Ah, here's our meal ticket." He rose, tugging Catherine up beside him, then wrapping his arm around her shoulders. "About time you made it back, old son. Catherine and I are starving, and you're buying lunch."

7

THEY ATE AT A SMALL French restaurant tucked away on a side street. San Francisco was full of small, interesting restaurants off the beaten path. Luke, who loved to eat as much as he loved to cook, knew them all.

It was fascinating to observe how people, men as well as women, were ogling her two escorts. Luke wore bright yellow suspenders over a collarless blue-and-white pinstripe shirt, navy Dockers and boat shoes, no socks. Nick was decked out in a double-breasted charcoal suit. Both looked hunky and gorgeous. Catherine felt like a thorn between two roses.

"Don't look now, Nick." She did an "over there" jerk of her chin. "But there's a sultry blonde at the table near the pillar who's about to fall out of her seat trying to get your attention."

"Actually—" Nick grinned without looking "—she's had my attention. It's Luke's attention she's trying to attract now."

Catherine's heart pinched. "How lovely. You share girlfriends. It must make life so much easier when you can give each other insider tips."

Luke shot a sidelong glance across the room.

"Want an intro, old son?" Nick murmured.

"Maybe later." Luke picked up his water glass,

drank deeply, then turned to Catherine. "What do you have planned for this afternoon?"

To see you in the middle of the day. "Shopping."

"What kind of shopping?" Nick asked. "If it's clothes, I'll go with you."

"Would you? That would be terrific, Nick, I'd lo—"

"You have an appointment at two, remember?" Luke reminded him. Nick looked blank. "You told me you were seeing...can't remember who it was, but someone."

"Huh? Oh. Yeah. Someone. Right."

"If you want company, Cat," Luke offered, "I've got the afternoon free. I can show you some good places to shop."

The fact that Luke, who loathed shopping, wanted to accompany her, and had outmaneuvered Nick, was grounds for celebration.

"I'd love you to come with me, Luke. I want to look for a couple of pairs of sandals."

She took a sip of coffee and caught Nick's eye over the rim of her cup. Those deep blue eyes challenged her.

"And underwear," she added casually.

"Underwear?" Luke repeated.

"Yeah, you know. Lingerie. The slinky stuff."

Nick rose, tossed his napkin on the table and stood behind Catherine's chair, his hand on her shoulder. "I'm devastated to miss this shopping trip. You know I love to shop. Catch you next time, Catherine." He squeezed her shoulder, then said to Luke, "I'm off to see Mrs. Somebody. Take care of my girl."

THANK GOD SHE DIDN'T model any of the stuff she was looking at. Luke would've had a stroke. As it was he was grateful to be sitting. He was as hard as petrified wood just watching Cat slide wispy bits of see-through silks and laces through her fingers before taking them into the dressing room. Surely to God none of those teddies would fit a grown woman? There wasn't more than five inches of fabric in the entire garment.

"You must be bored out of your mind." Cat emerged, a dozen satin hangers in each hand. Luke sat conspicuously on a spindly, peach-satin ladies' chair.

"I'm fine. Take your time." *I'm far too horny to stand or walk.* Luke dredged up a smile. "Really, Cat, I'm kinda enjoying the scenery. Take as long as you like." He'd never thought to frequent lingerie stores to troll for females. Too bad he couldn't care less about his new discovery. Cat glanced around, as if only now noticing the store was filled with women.

"Almost done. What do you think of these?"

"These" consisted of a bra that looked like two smiles of pale purple satin and a stamp-size sliver of supple, lime-green silk. There wasn't much to the top, and the bottom consisted of a short length of matching dental floss. There wasn't a single fluff of lace or frou-frou on either garment.

"Kinda plain, aren't they?" *Like wearing nothing at all.*

"I like the colors."

"Then buy them." She'd look like a mermaid, with a sexy, slippery wisp of green covering her long sexy, slippery body. The skimpy top would barely cover her breasts. Those delectable, peach tipped— "Buy them all and let's get out of here. You said you wanted shoes? There are a couple of reasonable places in the next block. I've got an appointment in a couple of hours. We'd better make tracks."

"But you said—"

"Hey, a man can only stand so much of a good thing."

Five hundred dollars worth of intimate apparel fit into a tiny shopping bag. The smaller the garment, apparently, the higher the price.

Luke felt much more himself when they walked into the shoe store. There was nothing remotely sexy about feet, in his opinion. His libido had taken a beating in the lingerie boutique. But now he could relax. He sat on one of the uncomfortable chairs lined up in the center of the store as Cat wandered around. That creamy yellow dress was dynamite on her; the color brought out the fire in her hair. Luke watched her through narrowed eyes. The simple style suited her; the square-necked, sleeveless dress had no waistline and gently fell to just above her knees, setting off long limbs lengthened by high heels.

Around her throat and draped between her breasts, Cat wore a heavy, almost barbaric necklace consisting of large cream and bronze beads and hammered copper squares. He'd bought the necklace and matching earrings and bracelet for her in Africa several years ago. At the time he'd imagined Cat wearing just that pagan jewelry. Nothing else. Instead of hand delivering his gift, Luke had mailed it to her in Oregon. Then he'd turned off the phone and got blind drunk for two days.

"Sorry. Are you in a coma?" Cat asked, giving him a sympathetic glance as she sat beside him. "I'd like to try these, please," she told the salesman hovering ingratiatingly nearby. She gave him her size and a handful of left shoes, and he trundled off.

Luke dredged up a smile and shifted slightly so they weren't quite so close. "I told you, I'm fine. Although I've got to admit I don't have the patience for shopping that Nick does. Man, that guy shops as enthusiastically as a woman. On the other hand, he never told me what a treasure trove lingerie shops are."

"Haven't you ever bought sexy lingerie for one of your girlfriends?"

"Hell, no!"

Cat laughed. "Why not?"

Luke was saved from answering by the salesman's return with several boxes, which he placed on the floor at Cat's feet like an offering. "I'll be back in a jiff," he assured her, then scurried off for more.

Luke didn't buy sexy lingerie for women. One, because he hated to shop, never went to malls, and frankly, it had never occurred to him to casually stroll into a potpourri-scented "pink" store. Two, because by the time he could order anything from a catalogue, the woman would have been long gone, only to be replaced by someone who might not be the same size.

He slouched in his chair. His knee brushed Cat's bare legs as he shifted. She smelled so damn good he wanted to forget the promises he'd made and lick her. All over. Then go back for seconds. And thirds...

The salesman knelt before Cat. "May I?" he asked,

removing the shoes from the box beside him and stripping out the paper stuffing. Catherine offered her foot.

The man slid on a high-heeled red sandal. "Oh, my. These shoes were made for you. Look how well they show off this glorious high arch of yours."

"Dream on," Luke grumbled under his breath.

The salesman cast him a wary glance as he produced the other damn shoe. Luke's mouth went Sahara dry. His eyes glommed on, riveted to her slender, tanned foot sliding slowly, slowly into that shoe. She had the sexiest feet he'd ever seen. High instep, neat little toes, nails painted a glossy fire-engine red. His erection had merely been lying dormant. It came back to life in a hurry. Oxygen drained out of his brain, leaving him dizzy.

Cat's feet were sexy as hell.

Who would've thunk it? he thought without humor. He wanted to slide those sandals on her himself. Luke closed his eyes. He pictured himself holding her heel in his palm, his other hand slipping the shoe slowly over her toes. Pictured his hand gliding up the smooth, lightly tanned, highly freckled length of her leg. Up. Up. To a wisp of a thong of lime-green silk—

"Well? What do you think?" Cat stood, wriggling her toes and looking down at him. Luke refocused and cleared his throat.

"Buy them in every color they have."

Cat frowned, then turned to the salesman. "Let me try on a few of the others."

While Cat and the man conferred on colors and styles, Luke congratulated himself on his fortitude and self sacrifice. He was a prince among men to resist her under so much temptation.

His eyes zeroed in on her sexy toes again.

Yeah, a saint.

CATHERINE SANG at the top of her voice as she walked into the living room fresh from a shower, rubbing her hair with a towel and heading for the kitchen. She screeched to a stop midnote when she saw Luke. He looked up from the book in his lap.

"Hey. You're home early," she said unnecessarily.

Grinning, he demanded, "What did you do with the money?"

"What money?"

"The money for the singing lessons."

"Ha ha. Spent it the same place you did those dancing lessons, Van Buren."

He wore white shorts and a tank top that had seen better days. He'd changed while she'd been in the bathroom, and had tossed the clothes he'd worn to work on the table by the front door. One of his shoes was near the bedroom door, the other under the coffee table. His socks decorated the lampshade.

"I had the bathroom door closed. You could have come in and changed in the bedroom, you know."

"Yeah, right," Luke said dryly. His eyes skimmed down the now damp cotton jersey of her sundress and back to her face.

They were having a heat wave. The most she could bear having next to her skin was the skimpy, bright yellow tank dress and cotton underwear. "Yeah, right?"

"Yeah. Right. I could have. But I didn't. Hey. Molly Cruz called. She wants you to call her back."

Catherine plucked his clothes off the table and lampshade and stood with the bundle in her arms. His shirt smelled so terrific she wanted to bury her nose in it. Luke sweat. She really was losing it.

"Thanks. I'll call her back tomorrow." She took his clothes into the bedroom and tossed them into the hamper.

Luke raised his voice through the open door. "Don't you miss your friends back home?"

"I talk to Molly, Susan and some of the others almost every other day, Luke." She came back pushing wet hair behind her shoulders, enjoying the coolness. "Which is pretty much what we've been doing for the last year or so, anyway. The distance hasn't made much difference."

"Yeah, but wasn't there someone special?"

Catherine frowned at him. What was she missing here? "Susan and Molly have been my best friends since second grade, you know that."

"A guy, Cat. A guy."

"No." She sank onto the sofa, curled her legs under her, stuffed one of the new cushions behind the small of her back, picked up *Sports Illustrated* from the coffee table to fan herself. The cool wet strands of her hair felt great slithering down her back. She swung her head, enjoying the sensation.

Luke stared at her, his eyes somewhat glazed. He cleared his throat. "What about a nipple?"

"A what?"

He looked blank for a second. "Nippon. You know.

A Japanese car. I was thinking you probably need a vehicle of some sort. Something small to drive around town. Easy to park. Good gas mileage on the freeway."

She could have sworn he'd said... God, she had sex on the brain. "I don't think I'll need a car, do you? If I want to go anywhere, I'll just take the bus or a cab."

"You can always use the Jag." He looked her up and down. "Heavy date tonight?"

"Nope. I'm in. You?"

"In." For a second she thought he'd go back to reading the book he clutched hard enough to whiten his knuckles. He looked up again. "Want to take in a nice air-conditioned movie?"

"You could have stopped at the words *air-conditioned*. I'd go anywhere cool right now. I had no idea San Francisco could get this hot." She uncurled her legs and rose to go to the kitchen. "I have yesterday's newspaper. Let's see what's on. As long as it's nothing with gushing blood," she added, as she returned with the paper and spread it out on the crowded coffee table.

"And nothing too schmaltzy," he warned as she crouched down to find the movie section. "Why don't you push the fishbowl and twenty-nine of those plants out of the way?"

"Cleo doesn't like to be moved," Catherine said, lifting the paper over the fishbowl and a thriving deffenbachia, and closer to Luke. She shifted so that she had to practically lean over his knees to see the print. "No vampires." She ran her hand through her wet hair. "Do you think Cleo is lonely?"

"Fish don't get lonely." He didn't move when she

rested an elbow on his knee, but he cleared his throat. "No costume dramas."

She wrapped an arm about his knee and leaned a little more of her weight against his leg. Rigor mortis set in as he froze.

Catherine pretended to watch Cleo blow bubbles and swim in circles as she settled comfortably against him. Her unfettered breast brushed against his bare knee.

"She looks lonesome to me. I think I'll buy her a friend tomorrow."

"Then b—" Luke cleared his throat. "Be prepared to be grandparent to a bunch of tadpoles."

Catherine laughed. "Fish have fish. Frogs have tadpoles."

"Same thing—"

"Not to the frogs and the fishies, it isn't."

"Keep the bowl in the bedroom then. I don't think I can handle fish procreation while I'm trying to watch CNN."

Interesting subject for Luke to bring up.

"And nothing too smoochie, either," he warned, before she could suggest the new romantic comedy at the Roxie.

Catherine pushed damp hair out of her face. "Jim Carrey?"

"What time?"

"Seven-fifteen." She used Luke's leg to lever herself to her feet. His thigh muscles flexed beneath her palm. "I have to dry my hair."

His gray-green eyes darkened. "And get dressed."

"I'm perfectly decent. Why can't I go like this?"

"Put on a bra."

Catherine hid her smile as she went off to dry her hair.

IT WASN'T A DATE.

But it sure felt like one to Luke. The theater was dark, and the movie, at any other time, would've captivated his attention.

Small problem: Catherine Anne Harris sat beside him. Close beside him. In the old theater, the seats were too narrow and far too close together. He'd had to extend his legs into the aisle to accommodate their length. Cat had to sit at an angle to accommodate hers. Which meant she was practically in his lap. She smelled of peach soap and popcorn, a fragrance Luke was rapidly becoming addicted to.

The huge tub of popcorn was on her lap. When he wanted to grab a handful his arm brushed her firm breast. Without looking at what she was doing, Cat fumbled for the giant soda he held on his own lap. Her fingers brushed his chest. He drew in a deep breath and handed her the paper cup.

"Thanks," she whispered against his cheek, eyes fixed on the screen. Her lips closed around the straw. Luke squeezed his eyes shut in self-defense. He imagined those lips closing around him.

"I'm going out," he whispered harshly. "Be right back."

LUKE PULLED OPEN THE DOOR to the men's room. He couldn't handle this. Could. Not. Handle. This.

He sat in a stall and stared at the graffiti on the back

of the door. He wanted Cat. No. He more than wanted her. He'd desired women before. But what he felt for Cat...what he felt for Cat was deeper, more complex. Just more, dammit! That wasn't going to go away. In fact, if anything, it was getting worse by the minute.

He couldn't concentrate at work. He wasn't getting any sleep. His appetite was shot to hell. Luke felt the familiar tug-of-war he'd been experiencing for years—his own need balanced with honor. Half of him wanted to come right out and show Cat how much he wanted her. The other half remembered what a tender heart she had, how easily she could be hurt.

Been there, done that.

The night of her seventeenth birthday party came to mind. And the sharp sting of his father's disapproval as he'd yelled, "Don't go thinking you can use that girl to scratch an itch! She's not her mother. Catherine is a forever woman."

His father had been more furious than Luke had ever seen him. "What would you do with a girl like Catherine once you had her?"

The accurate punch of that statement hit him square on the jaw. What he wanted to do and what his own moral code demanded he do were polar opposites.

He was a man who thrived on sampling.

Catherine Anne Harris was a keeper.

The promise to always be her big brother hadn't been made lightly. His depth of sincerity had been in direct proportion to the hurt and anguish he'd inflicted on her. He wouldn't renege on that now. Even if Cat was sharpening her inexperienced claws on his heart right now, he couldn't go back on his word. He went through The Promise about thirty-nine times in his mind. Bottom line? He'd promised himself and his dad that he would take care of Cat.

Taking care of Cat meant putting her best interests ahead of his own. Ahead of his marauding testosterone, his own lust, his own desires. He was a mature adult, not a hormone driven adolescent. He could deny himself; he could control his base urges. No one had ever died of lust, as far as he knew. He resigned himself to being horny for however long it took Cat to find what she was looking for. When she was settled he could take care of his own physical needs.

Luke didn't want to consider why he couldn't take care of those needs while seeing to Cat's happiness. The two seemed somehow entwined in his mind. If he couldn't have Cat, he didn't want anyone else. Frustrated, but determined to stick to the letter of the law, he groaned.

From the next stall, someone pounded on the dividing wall. "Get yourself a girl, mister!"

8

LUKE WAS IN THE KITCHEN scraping burned cookies into the garbage disposal when Cat returned home from her date with Dan the following night.

"Phew-ee!" Catherine waved her hands. "That is *mucho* stinky! What are you still doing up?"

"Burning cookies. How was your date?"

Catherine sat on a bar stool and swung her foot. "Fun. The play was terrific. We ate at a fabulous little Italian place off the beaten track called Giovanni's. Do you know it?"

"I was the one who told him about it. You and old Daniel hit it off, huh?"

"Umm. He's charming."

"Just remember, he's been married once before."

"No problem, as long as he doesn't bring his ex to dinner with us," Catherine said cheerfully.

"Devil's food cake?"

"Nah. Strawberry swirl."

THIS WAS NOT GOING WELL, she decided several days later. One of the problems was she was rarely home. The other was...well, she was being too subtle. She needed to turn up the heat. They were anchored out on the Bay on Nick's twenty-seven-foot sailboat. Even at six in the evening, the heat of the day was oppressive.

She felt like the Wicked Witch in *The Wizard of Oz*. *Melt*ing.

There wasn't a breath of wind, the dark blue water reflected mirror smooth, the air shimmered. Dozens of white-sailed boats, manned by scantily clad people hoping for an ocean breeze, cruised the Bay. In the distance the city looked freshly washed and as picture perfect as a postcard. She could even see the twin towers of their condo beyond Marina Green.

Luke lay sprawled facedown on a towel on the varnished deck. Nick slouched on a folding deck chair, a book on his chest, eyes closed. Both wore swimsuits and a light film of perspiration on their tanned skins.

Catherine, wearing a soft lime-green sundress, and sitting in the shade, sighed. She pulled the light T-shirt fabric farther up her bare legs. "Do you think if I sit in the sun my freckles will join together and I'll get a nice even tan?"

"You've been asking me that same question since you turned fifteen," Luke told her. "And the answer is still no." He reached blindly for the soda beside him. Catherine nudged it closer with her toe.

"Thanks. Remember when you went to Hawaii that year? You came back parboiled and peeling."

"How do you know? You weren't there." That was the year he'd gone to the Pratt Institute in New York to study architecture. She'd felt as though a cannonball had gone through her chest and left a gaping, bleeding hole. Worse even than the day her mom had walked out and left her behind.

"Dad told me about it."

Catherine felt her eyes well, and bit her lip. She'd

had wonderful years with her stepfather. Good years. She had to remember those. But, God, how she missed him. Missed the unconditional love he'd always given her. Missed the feel of his arms around her. Missed that safety and the sense of belonging he'd provided. She closed her eyes and said a quick prayer of gratitude for the years they had shared.

"Hey." Luke curled his fingers around her ankle. His hand was cold from holding the soda can as he absently smoothed his thumb up and down her anklebone. "Dad wouldn't have wanted you to be sad on such a beautiful day."

"How did you know I was thinking about him?" Icy hot shivers sheeted her skin at his touch.

"Your mouth always goes soft and sort of pouty when you're sad. Come on, Catwoman. Give me a smile."

Thankful her sunglasses hid her misty eyes, Catherine felt her heart expand as she looked down at him lying there like a giant sun-loving lion. Miles of smooth, tanned, naked skin; sweat-dampened dark hair; heartbreaking smile.

"Good memories," she said around the lump in her throat.

"I know," Luke said softly. Although she couldn't see his eyes behind his glasses, she could feel his gaze skim her face. He let go of her ankle and she felt bereft.

"It was just one of those quick, sneaky whammies. I'm getting better every day."

"Isn't that a song?"

"Yes. But please spare us and don't sing it."

"Hear, hear," Nick agreed, reminding them he was also on board.

The muscles in Luke's back flexed as he pillowed his head on his hands. "Man, this is the life. I could get used to it."

A seagull squawked as it wheeled lazily overhead. Wavelets lapped the wooden hull; lines creaked. The boat barely moved. The scent of suntan lotion overrode the salty tang of the water.

If she leaned down and stretched out her hand, she could touch Luke's shoulder. Catherine wanted to touch him so badly her fingernails tingled. Her heart sped up and her palms felt slick on her soda can. She imagined sliding her hands up his back, drawing his half naked body against hers. She imagined Luke blocking out the sun as he angled his head to kiss her, imagined his mouth touching hers....

Imagined him wanting her.

Not like the last disastrous time she'd kissed him, nine years ago. She'd almost knocked him to the floor in her exuberance. What a naive fool she'd been. Of course he'd been repulsed. Even inebriated, she'd known how appalled Luke had been. After several Keystone Cops moves, Luke had managed to extricate himself from her rubbery hold with a firm, no-nonsense grip of her shoulders. Then he'd yelled at her. Or had she thrown up and then he'd yelled at her? She shuddered at the memory.

But that was then, this was now. Luke wasn't going anywhere. She wasn't feeling cool linoleum under her bare feet, but the solid wood deck. She wasn't a beer-giddy, euphoric seventeen-year-old. She was stone cold sober.

No time like the present. Her heart did an anticipatory jig in her chest. The can made a little popping sound as she squeezed it too tightly.

"Okay. Which of you is the best kisser?" she asked into the heat-induced silence.

"I am," both men said in unison. Luke lifted his glasses off his nose, opened one eye and squinted up at her. "Why?"

"Because I think I need kissing lessons."

"Good idea," Nick said, using a water-filled plastic spray bottle to spritz his legs and chest. He gave Catherine a wink of approval. She kept her expression bland.

"Bad idea. Bad, bad idea." Luke scowled at Nick. "She does not need kissing lessons. Don't encourage her."

"Gee, I'm sorry you don't approve." Catherine peered at him over her sunglasses. "But I'm serious here. This is a skill I want to master. I've heard kissing can be taken to a fine art. I've had the sloppy kind, the dry kind, the icky kind and pretty much everything in between. I want to be taught by the best. So I can even the playing field. Who's it going to be?" She avoided looking directly at Luke while she spoke, lest she chicken out.

"We'll both teach you, Catherine," Nick said. "You'll have the advantage of learning from two masters."

"Forget it." Luke sat up. He had the imprint of the towel on his sweat-sheened chest. "Women are born knowing how to seduce. We should be teaching her what to expect and how to resist. Martial arts. That's what we should be teaching her, for heaven's sake! Besides, Cat's not having two men stick their tongues down her throat one after the other. That's gross."

"Oh, thank you for sparing me that. Sticking your tongue down my throat? If that's how you two turkeys exhibit finesse, I'd rather kiss a frog."

"No frogs in saltwater." Nick reached for his shorts lying on the deck under his chair. "If you learn from a master, you won't waste your time kissing a bunch of horny toads. Hey, old son, I'll flip you for it." He took a coin out of a pocket.

Luke look horrified. "You can't flip a coin for something as intimate as a kiss."

"Sure we can. Remember Jennifer?"

"That was different."

Knowing the coin Nick held was double-sided, Catherine hid a smile. "Oh, just ignore him and flip it," she instructed Nick. She shot Luke a glance. "If I don't mind, why should you?"

"Call." Nick prepared to flip.

"Forget it." Luke scowled. "Neither of us is teaching Cat anything. When the right man comes along, he'll do all the teaching she wants. Until then, keep your grubby lips to yourself, Stratton."

"Catherine?" Nick asked.

She shrugged. "If Luke doesn't want to help, then I'd welcome any pointers you can give me. Thanks, Nick."

Nick gave her a sexy, dimpled smile and held out his hand. "Stand up, sweetheart, and let's see what I can do."

"Stay right where you are, Cat."

"Don't be such a grouch." Catherine rose, stepped over him and took Nick's hand. "Okay, how should we do this?"

"Put your mouth anywhere near hers and you'll be fish bait." Luke jerked upright. "And take your hand off her butt."

Catherine struggled to keep a straight face. She couldn't even look at Nick as he carefully lifted his hand from the small of her back.

"One of us is going to help Catherine out, old son." Nick tugged her against his side. "Why don't you go below for an hour or so? I don't want an audience. Do you, Catherine?"

Don't overdo it, Nick. "Not particularly, no."

Luke ignored her to glare at his friend. "An hour? She wants a kissing lesson, not a detailed road map through the *Kama Sutra*."

Nick pulled her closer. "Anything worth doing is worth doing well."

"No."

"Hey, you had a chance to call it. Either of us would do, right, Catherine?"

"Heads," Luke snapped.

"Damn, I was really looking forward to—"

"Flip the damn coin."

Nick grinned, slid Cat a wink and flipped the coin. It caught the sunset as it spun head over head and onto the back of his hand. He slapped his palm down, then lifted it to look. "Heads it is. Should I close my eyes, or would you prefer I go below and take my time finding something cold to drink?"

"How about swimming back to the marina via Alaska?"

"Luke!"

Nick laughed. "Man, you're a sore winner. I'm off to find some compelling reason to stay below." He quirked an eyebrow at Luke. "Unless you want me to stay and coach from the sidelines?"

"I certainly don't need coaching, but there's no need to make yourself scarce. This'll only take a minute."

"A minute?" Nick gave her a sympathetic look. "Poor Catherine, being instructed by someone with such a limited repertoire. Let me—"

"For a man who couldn't even dredge up a date for tonight, you're a fine one to talk," Luke told him sourly.

"I had a date tonight, old son. There she is. About to be mashed by my best friend. Go figure how I ended up being the third wheel."

I'm damned if I do and damned if I don't, Luke thought as Nick went below. Luke dragged on heavy jeans shorts over his thin swimsuit—the closest thing to body armor he could come up with at such short notice. He shifted his stance so he could pull up the zipper.

"What on earth are you doing?" Cat asked as she flopped into a chair. "You're going to roast alive in those hot things."

True. On the other hand, he was already on high boil just looking at her and imagining his lips on her mouth.

"I don't want to get you overexcited. Stand up."

Cat grinned. She rose from the chair and reached up

to hold on to the rigging to keep her balance. It was a centerfold stance, with one slender arm curved over her head, the other at her side. The soft fabric of her dress molded nicely to the gentle swell of her breasts and clung to her hips and long legs.

"Overexcited? By a little kiss? Oh, puh-leeze. Get real."

Ahh. Fighting words. A challenge if he ever heard one. Unfortunately, this was one he'd prefer not to accept.

Kiss Cat? Touch his mouth to hers? Feel her breath? Man. This was a bad idea. Bad, bad idea. Look what had happened the last time. He had to refuse.

The words hovered like something bitter on the tip of his tongue. *Just say no*, he told himself. But he saw the tantalizing sparkle in her amber eyes, the joyous lift of her lips. The knowledge he read in her face—that no matter what she asked of him, he'd come through for her—dissolved his resistance.

He was doomed.

"How do you feel?" he asked cautiously.

Her eyes opened wide. "Just fine. Why?"

"Tummy okay?"

Their eyes met as they both remembered that night. Her chin came up; her amber eyes dared him. "I'm feeling in the pink of good health. Smooch away."

Accustomed to the gentle pitch of the boat, he strolled over to stand in front of her, then gave her a reproving look.

"You have to concentrate here, Cat. There are kisses and then there are kisses. I'll show you how it's supposed to be done. But you have to close your eyes and focus on the subtle nuances." Which would be a nice change from the last time he'd mangled her lips in a fit of misplaced passion.

Tiger eyes alight with mirth, Cat looked up at him. "Subtle nuances? You?"

"Remove your hat and glasses, please," he instructed sternly. He could make this a quick tutorial. He didn't have to get involved. It was just a kiss. Two sets of lips touching briefly. Nothing to it.

Cat dutifully pulled off the baseball cap she'd been wearing and tossed it down the companionway. Freed from the confines of the hat, her hair went berserk. An explosion of shiny Titian-red curls demanded to be crushed beneath his fingers. Luke kept his marauding fingers and itchy palms at his sides.

She removed her sunglasses and glanced around for somewhere safe to put them. He plucked them from her, whipped off his own shades and set both on the chair she'd just vacated. He straightened and scrutinized her face. The anticipation was going to kill him. But now, when he suddenly had the opportunity to show her...whatever it was he wanted to show her, he was scared spitless.

He saw in her eyes the memory of another kiss. Another challenge. But the only miserable consolation about that disastrous night had been Cat's claim to have only vague memories about what had happened. Thank God. He didn't want those memories to taint this. Which was just a simple kiss.

He was delusional. This wasn't just a kiss. He knew that. His body knew that. He just didn't want Cat to know it. He felt the thud of his heart deep in his chest.

Felt the tightening of his jeans. Felt a rush of desire so strong, so profound he simply stood there, riding the gentle buck of the waves, and looked down at her.

"How long are you going to stand there staring at me?" she demanded, chin out, eyes bright. She narrowed those witchy eyes, and Luke knew he was on a slippery slope wearing wet, leather-soled shoes.

"In a hurry?"

"Well, no..."

He reached up and anchored her fingers on the rigging with his own. His hand covered hers completely. Slowly, he slid his right hand under her hair to cup the back of her damp neck. The filaments clung to his hand and arm like living flame. A pulse throbbed a jungle beat in his ears. The universe around them bled into soft focus, leaving Cat in sharp relief before him. Beautiful Cat. *His* Cat.

He was going to have to make this a lasting memory.

"You have to take a breath," he reminded her, noticing she'd stopped inhaling completely when he touched her. Her breasts brushed his chest as she drew in a shaky breath.

"Right."

Her green dress wasn't particularly low cut. Luke could just see the freckled swell of her breasts above the fabric. But the thought of that soft material hiding her luscious breasts almost had him in cardiac arrest. She took another shuddery breath, and he caught a glimpse of shiny lime-green silk.

That teddy thing she'd bought the other day. Slick green silk over bare skin. That thong riding between her legs... His fingers tightened imperceptibly on her nape. She tilted her face.

He lowered his head and touched his mouth to the pulse at her temple, and felt her slight start of surprise as he feathered his lips on the unsteady flutter he discovered there. He made soothing noises as his lips traveled across her cheek. Discovered the taste of her skin. Gauged her response to the lightest of touches. He ran the tip of his tongue experimentally across the eyelashes on her left eye. She murmured under her breath. He duplicated the action on her other lid. Her breath huffed out against his throat.

Luke shuddered as her hand crept around his waist. He removed it and patted it to her side, then lifted his mouth a fraction. "That's lesson number...later. Hold your horses, woman." He went back to her eyelids.

"Umm."

Oh, yeah, more than umm.

Her skin felt incredibly soft and smooth under his exploring mouth. He imagined the heady taste of cinnamon as his lips skimmed across her hot cheek, the end of her nose, the other cheek. Cat's fingers flexed restlessly under his on the ropes. Her breasts brushed lightly against his bare chest as she started to lean into him again. He shifted out of reach, dry tinder eluding the gasoline-drenched torch.

"Nuh-uh," he teased, already as hard as the mast.

His lips brushed the corner of her mouth. She made a strangled, yearning sound low in her throat. Luke resisted the primitive urge to crush her beneath him and take her right there beneath the sunny sky, out on deck.

Cool your jets. He didn't want to scare her away. Not now. Not when he was so close to heaven.

They touched in only three places: their fingers gripping the rigging, his hand on her nape and the butterfly-light touch of his mouth on hers. Yet his entire body seemed sensitized by her close proximity. Her breath smelled of the Dr. Pepper she'd been drinking. Sweet, spicy. *Cat. Ahh, Cat.* Just what the doctor ordered. Too bad he was on a restricted diet.

Luke angled his head slightly and nipped her lower lip with his teeth. She nibbled back. He laved the bites with his tongue. She licked his lip like a frustrated, hungry cat. He brushed his mouth back and forth over hers. She hummed and parted her lips. Luke settled his mouth on hers. Her lips responded automatically, melding with his, anticipating the shift and slide of his tongue.

He was inside.

The scented flavor of her mouth tasted achingly familiar. Luke had imagined this for so long, it felt like coming home. He shuddered as desire, hot, strong and pounding, surged through his body like a drug. He felt dizzy with it. High. Ridiculously, disproportionately happy from one tame little kiss.

But it wasn't tame. It was hot. Wild. Surging.

Teeth, tongues, lips, melding together in a mind-blowing kiss hot enough to evaporate the water of the Bay.

Brake. Brake. Brake.

Luke lifted his head and broke contact. "That should do it."

She looked up at him, eyes dazed, lips damp, cheeks pink.

"Hmm, not bad." She seemed to shake herself out of a fog as she stumbled back a step. "I wonder how Nick does it."

IT WAS THE NIGHT AFTER The Kiss.

Catherine snuggled back into the squishy cushions on Nick's sofa, ignoring the movie they were watching. She closed her eyes, picturing Luke's face after The Kiss. Annoyance? Shock at her brazenness? His expression had been impossible to read.

Twenty-four hours later, she still felt the jolt that kiss had given her heart. She wished she could bottle the sensation and take it out in the dark of night to hug close. She'd never felt such a weird mixture of peace and agitation in her life.

It was exactly as if she had come home. As if she had stood outside, shivering in the snow, looking into the window at everything she'd ever wanted in her life. It was all right there at her fingertips. All she had to do was reach out and grab it.

Unfortunately, he'd suddenly remembered he had a date. They'd sped back to the marina, Nick cranky because Luke insisted he use the motor instead of the sail. Luke had rushed into the condo, showered, changed and raced out as if the hounds of hell were nipping at his heels.

Catherine had lied and told him she had a date, too. Then spent several boring hours sitting through a subtitled German movie staring at the back of some Luke-lookalike's head before dragging herself home.

Despite a restless, sleepless night, she hadn't heard his return. But this morning when she'd left to go out for a while he was sound asleep on the sofa.

Catherine touched her lips. How odd that they felt and looked just the same. When Luke had touched his mouth to hers last night, something inside her had shifted and stirred. Changed. She'd literally felt like Sleeping Beauty awakening from a deep sleep. And she realized she hadn't known what love was until now.

She'd been so blinded by the sheer sexy maleness of Lucas Van Buren that she hadn't noticed herself tumbling headlong into a forever kind of love.

She'd made an eyes-wide-open decision to give herself one last chance at seeing if what she felt could possibly be reciprocated. But she was a realist. Luke wasn't ever going to settle down. What if she got what she wanted? Could she walk away when it was over? *Be careful what you wish for. You might get it.*

Yes. Because the alternative was never knowing, always aching, spending the rest of her life empty and unfulfilled. Something with Luke was better than everything with somebody else. And when it was inevitably over, she'd have the memory of Luke's heat to keep her warm.

Catherine hugged a cushion. Insecurity squeezed her chest. Luke had sure been in one big old hurry to get away from her last night. It had been more subtle than nine years ago only because he had more finesse now. Was she doing irreparable damage to what she already had with him? Perhaps she should leave well enough alone. Luke cared for her; she knew he did.

Maybe that should be enough. If she got too greedy, she took the chance of losing it all.

"Hey, Nick?"

With a grin, Nick pointed the remote control at the TV and the sound went off. "Wanna analyze The Kiss?"

She squeezed the cushion to her aching middle. "Let's."

"Scared?"

"Spitless," Catherine admitted. "He sped out of there last night like his hair was on fire. How was he at work today?"

"Like his hair was on fire." Nick's dimples showed. Easy for him to be amused. "You were priceless yesterday, honey. Trust me. The fish might be struggling on the hook, but you just have to be strong enough to hang on to that line."

"I'm terrified. I don't want to force him. I just want— I want..."

"Him to love you as much as you love him." He gave her a sympathetic look. "Luke's a hard nut, you know that. He's got this protective instinct a mile wide."

"The last thing I want is for him to feel obligation."

"Catherine, he can't help feeling some obligation to take care of you. He's pretty much your only family. It's not in Luke's nature to turn his back."

Her frown turned to a scowl, and her heart felt like a heavy rock in her chest. "Are you telling me Luke is humoring me because of some asinine sense of responsibility?"

"No. I'm telling you Luke thinks he's humoring you because he feels responsible for you."

"Huh? Isn't that the same thing?"

"No, it isn't." Nick picked up a cold slice of pizza out of the box beside him. "Luke wants you, Catherine. Trust me on this. I know my pal. He's about to shed his skin, he wants you so bad. He's resisting the pull with every particle of his willpower. And as we both know, Luke has awesome willpower. Remember when he gave up smoking? Cold turkey. And when we bet we wouldn't drink beer for a month? It was on our first college break. I caved in two weeks. Despite winning, Luke stuck it out the exact thirty days."

"If he wants me," Catherine said, completely frustrated, "why doesn't he just...have me? Why resist? What's the point? I'm here, I'm available. I want him. Dammit, Nick. Why?"

"Have you noticed what type of woman our friend dates?"

"Sure," Catherine said miserably. "Petite blondes, miniature brunettes. Boobs out to here. And of course, all of them are sexy and beautiful. Why do men always have to go for a 'type,' anyway?"

"Other than the sexy and beautiful part, which you are, have you ever noticed how much his type doesn't resemble you?"

Catherine sank her chin into the cushion she was clutching. "Oh, great! Thanks for pointing that out."

"He'll date anyone as long as she doesn't resemble you. Interesting, huh?"

"That isn't an answer, and I think this conversation just took a useless U-turn."

"I'm just reminding you of Luke Van Buren's amazing self-control and willpower. Which he has to spare. Not to mention he's as stubborn as a mule. It's taking him longer than I thought to separate the woman from The Kid. Personally, I've always thought he dated The Many to keep him safe from The One." Before he could explain what that meant, he was interrupted by a loud banging at the front door. Nick glanced up and grinned. "Speak of the devil."

9

BAM, BAM, BAM.

It sounded like the fire department responding to a five-alarm blaze. If it was Luke out there, he was about to pound down the door. Catherine sat up from her reclining position on the sofa and curled bare legs under her. She and Nick looked at each other and grinned in perfect harmony.

Bam. Bam. Bam.

"Yo, Nick? You home?"

Bam. Bam.

Nick turned off the lamp, quickly lit the three candles on the coffee table, then came up beside her chair and ruffled her hair so it flip-flopped wildly around her head.

"Rub your lips. Hard," he instructed, before yelling, "Hey! I'm coming, cool your jets!"

"Where were you? Peru?" Luke demanded, almost falling inside the room when Nick opened the door. "Is Cat—there you are." He gave a suspicious glance around. "Why's it so cold and dark in here?"

"Nick bought an air conditioner. Great, huh?"

"What'd it do? Suck up all the electricity?" Luke came farther into the room. One glance took in the flickering candles, their wineglasses, the pillows piled up on the end of the sofa. Another glance took in her shorts and tank top. The third bulletlike look zeroed in on her red, swollen lips. He frowned. His glance shot down to her chest, where her nipples were hard from the cold.

"How was your 'business' dinner?" Cat inquired, stretching out her bare legs on Nick's chenille sofa. She tried for an innocent-but-really-guilty look.

"The client was enthusiastic." Obviously Luke wasn't going to notice her facial expression at the moment. He was still glaring at her chest.

"I just bet she was," Cat mumbled, appalled at the apple-green jealousy she was experiencing. "Want a glass of wine?" she asked, reaching for the sweating bottle in the ice bucket.

"Your mother's on the phone."

She shot him a startled look. "My mother?"

"On the phone. Upstairs."

"You put Catherine's mother on hold while you came down here?" Nick sat on the arm of the sofa, then rested his hand on her shoulder. "Where's she calling from?"

"Didn't ask."

Catherine rose and searched for her sandals. "Last time I heard, she was in Portugal." She slipped her feet into them. "She didn't call collect, did she?"

"No." He pinched the bridge of his nose. "Go see what she wants, and then say no, okay?"

She pushed her hair out of her face. "Sure," she said dryly, then turned to her host. "Thanks for a fun evening, Nick."

"Want me to put...the movie on pause till you get back?"

Catherine smiled. She couldn't look at Luke, but she sensed a scowl. "No. But hold that thought. We'll finish...what we started another time, okay?"

"I'll be here," Nick told her, sounding sincere and extremely disappointed. He briefly touched her cheek with bent knuckles as she walked by him.

"I'll come back upstairs with you," Luke told her firmly, walking between them to sling his arm around her shoulders and herd her toward the door.

"Give me a few minutes first, okay?"

"Sure." At the front door he took her chin in his palm. A shiver traveled through Catherine's body. "Remember, no is a complete sentence. If you use it enough, Faith might get it."

Not likely. "I'll be fine. Thanks, Luke."

HE FOUND HER STANDING outside on the patio when he came upstairs fifteen minutes later.

"How'd it go?" he asked, stepping through the sliding door and walking up beside her where she stood at the railing. The phone lay on the table behind her, next to the fishbowl, which she must have brought out for company.

His patio used to hold two canvas-cushioned loungers, a low plastic table and several empty beer cans. It now gave every appearance of being the set for an Amazon movie. A veritable jungle of flowering plants and vines vied for space with clay pots filled with flowers and a forest of candles of various heights and sizes. All it needed was a swooping parrot.

She hadn't turned on the overhead light, but the lights from inside were bright enough for him to observe her pale face and the stiff set of her lips. Cat wasn't a crier. Not on the outside, anyway.

"She's getting married again," she told the stars.

"Aw, Cat." Luke casually slung an arm around Cat's shoulders as they stared out at the twinkling lights ringing the Bay. She leaned against him slightly, and he ran his hand down her smooth arm. Down. Up. Down. Mindful of her brittleness, he angled his head toward hers and rested his chin on her crown. Her hair smelled of lemons and fire, and it felt as soft as a kitten's fur where it brushed his chin.

"I kinda figured that when she didn't call collect this time." Faith always called collect when she needed money. Or a place to stay. Or sympathy. The woman was an emotional vampire.

Man, he was in big trouble when the fragrance of Cat's hair turned him on. "When's the wedding?"

"Next week. This one's in Arizona. She wants me to be a bridesmaid again."

"How maternal of her. And how like her to tell you at the eleventh hour, then expect you to hotfoot it to her side."

Cat turned her head to glance up at him. Her frenetic hair brushed the back of his arm, sending a nice little burst of electricity up his nerve endings. "It's only a weekend. No big deal. I'm used to Faith by now."

"No kidding. This is what? Number nine?"

"This is the man she's been looking for all her life." Cat's hands clenched the wrought-iron railing. Luke felt the muscles in her arm bunch under the pressure. He stroked her skin until the muscles relaxed. "She sounded happy, at least," Cat said quietly.

"He must be loaded."

"So she said. His name is Chandler Roberts. He's her plastic surgeon."

"Convenient. She'll keep him busy. Are you going to play bridesmaid again?"

"Sure." Cat's voice was dry. "I firmly believe every woman should have a closet full of froufrou dresses."

"You aren't the froufrou type."

"Really?" She looked up at him. "What type am I?"

Gentle. Loving. Sexy as hell. "Practical. Sensible. Down-to-earth."

"Thanks." The corners of her soft mouth turned down. "In other words, not in the least little bit like my mother."

"Who is...what?" Luke asked cautiously.

"Sexy, vivacious, beautiful."

"Try obvious, loud, surgically enhanced. The woman's a walking cliché."

Cat smiled. "You have a way with words, Van Buren. Will you come to the wedding with me?"

"Don't I always?"

She smiled, her eyes shiny. "I'm going inside for ice water. Want some?"

"No, thanks. Bring the cookies when you come back."

Luke wanted to get Faith Harris-Ford-Van Buren-Davis - Turner - Collingswod - Ashby - Landry - soon - to-be-Roberts in a room alone for about ten minutes for a reality check. Cat, thank God, seemed to be well enough adjusted. Her mother's frequent marriages were met with calm stoicism. However, Luke suspected Cat's nonchalant veneer was only skin-deep.

How couldn't it not hurt her to see her mother choose one man after the other, with no thought, no consideration for her only child? It amazed him that Cat would even consider marriage.

He'd known, even as a kid, that marriage wasn't for him. The thought had always left him cold. Nothing lasted as long as both parties wanted. Someone was doomed to be destroyed. And even if, by some chance, the adults withdrew relatively unscathed, the poor kid left in the middle was always devastated.

After the divorce, his mom had held on to him so tightly he'd sometimes wished he'd had Cat's problem. He remembered lying in bed listening to his mother sob for hours. Even though she'd remarried, she'd never gotten over the divorce from his father. Luke couldn't imagine how Faith did it repeatedly.

Cat returned carrying a large glass of ice-clinking water and the plate of chocolate chip cookies he'd baked the night before when she'd been out with some guy she'd met running in the park. Brian something-or-other. An unknown quantity and therefore dangerous.

Luke sprawled out on one of the canvas covered loungers and held out his hand for the plate. Cat walked around the low table to sit beside him. She set the cool plate down on his stomach, then took a sip of her water.

They both wore shorts, and her bare leg pressed against his, sending a spear of electricity up his thigh directly into his groin. She smelled of some spicy-sweet powder, a fragrance Luke had associated with her for years.

He wanted to interrogate her about the scene he'd just witnessed downstairs. He wanted to discuss, coolly and clinically, the inadvisability of yesterday's kiss. He wanted to politely request she move off his lounger and sit over there, a comfortable three feet away, where he wouldn't be forced to touch her. But her mouth was pouty, her eyes a little sad, her shoulders not quite straight. He couldn't withdraw his emotional support just because he was having a hard time keeping his hands off her.

"Want to talk about it?" he asked gently.

Cat fished in her glass for a large piece of ice. "Same old, same old." She blew out a huff of air, ruffling her bangs. "Doesn't it ever cool off around here? What happened to the San Francisco breezes I'm always hearing about?"

No breeze was going to cool him off. His concentration was shot, intent on erotic, inappropriate thoughts. Like how soft her skin looked. Like how delicious her lips had tasted yesterday. Like how good she smelled.

"They say the heat will stick around for another couple of days before it slacks off. We could always get an air conditioner." And what had been going on downstairs earlier with Nick?

"No. I can stand it for a while." She ran the ice down her throat, leaving a trail of moisture on her skin, then tilted her head and slowly drew the cube down the side of her neck. The muscles in Luke's stomach clenched, and he had to force rational words through a constriction in his throat.

"What's she trying to entangle you with this time?"

"She doesn't really try to involve me in her life. She

only calls when..." Cat waved a dismissive hand. "Hey, that's fine with me. I figured out years ago that what Faith does, and how she does it, has nothing to do with me."

Luke dragged his gaze away from the gleam of moisture on her throat. "What else did she have to say for herself?"

"She'd just returned from Paris." Cat smiled. "She has a French accent this time. She told me it took a month to purchase her trousseau. Just the thought of shopping that long gives me hives."

"Did she by any chance ask how you were doing?"

"Sure. She asked if I was using the face cream she'd had custom blended for me in Germany. I said absolutely." Cat grinned. "I didn't mention I'd used it all on the neighbors' poor little dog when it had eczema a few months ago."

"Good for you. You don't need any fancy lotions and potions on your skin." Luke's gaze followed the shiny trail of water across the smooth skin on Cat's collarbone. He licked his lips.

"I d-don't?"

"No. Did you kiss Nick tonight?" Luke asked, his voice husky.

"Nick?"

"My business partner. The guy you spent the evening with?" Oh, man. He'd lost his freaking mind. He couldn't even concentrate on a simple conversation because he couldn't think of anything other than his hands trailing that ice. His hands on her skin. His touch making her nipples peak like that. What was he doing? Playing with fire. No, worse. Dynamite. He was playing with volatile, incendiary nitroglycerine. Get your mind off sex. Now.

"Hmm? Oh, Nick. Uh-uh." Drops of water trickled down her chest to moisten the edge of her tank top. "Aren't you hot?"

"Hell, yes, I'm hot!" Need clawed at him. "Go sit over there. No more touchy-feely, Cat, you're getting me sweaty."

He swung his legs over the other side of the lounger. "Look, if none of the guys I've introduced you to so far have rung your chimes, there are a couple more we can tr—"

Cat made a rude noise. "Don't bother. Your selection's been more than ample. I've found my Mr. Right."

Luke put a finger to his throat. Yep. He still had a pulse. "Who," he asked dangerously, "is he?"

"I'd rather not say right now. Just in case—"

"Just in case?" Luke raked his fingers through his hair until it stood up like a cockscomb. "Cat, if this is Mr. Right, you should be absolutely positive. Are you positive?"

"Oh, yes." She picked up the half-filled glass at her feet and took a long slug of tepid water. "Before I do anything, though, I'd like you to give me some pointers." She sent him a guileless look. "Your input will be invaluable, because—because he's very much like you."

"Like me?"

"You know. Suave. Cool. Sophisticated. A ladies' man."

Luke felt as though he'd just bitten into a quince. "A player."

Catherine smiled. "Exactly. If anyone can tell me how to seduce a player, you'd be the one."

Luke shot off the lounger and paced to the patio railing, his back ramrod stiff. After several heart-stopping minutes he turned to face her. "Are you out of your ever-loving mind, Catherine Harris? Which one is he?"

"I told you, I don't want to tell y—"

"Is he someone I know?"

"Jeez, Luke, what difference does it make? I'm certainly old enough to have an affair and intelligent enough to know when I'm ready for one."

He scowled. "I thought this was Mr. Right? You don't have an affair with Mr. Right, Cat. You marry him. *Marry.* Until death do you part."

"I'm sure the people across the Bay are taking notes. You don't have to shout. And he won't marry me. He has noncommittalitis, just like you do."

"You want marriage. You're a Cancer. Cancers nest. Home and hearth and all that stuff."

"Well, I'll be happy just having him. I can live without the trappings."

"No, Catherine. You cannot. Besides, you said you wanted to find a husband."

"It's my prerogative to change my mind. Now I want a lover."

"I know you—"

"Not as well as you thought, obviously. Stop grinding your teeth like that, you'll wear down the enamel. I can't imagine any sophisticated man would be interested in teaching some little hick virgin the finer points of making love, can you? Now, will you give me the help I need or not?"

"Cat..." Luke pressed his hands into his temples. "A man lives to be a woman's first. It's a fantasy few men fulfill."

"Weird, huh?" Catherine crossed her legs and leaned back on the lounger Luke had vacated. "A man wants to be a woman's first. And every woman wants to be a man's last."

He pressed his fingers into his throbbing eye sockets.

"What's the prob?" Cat taunted. "Don't think you can?"

"Can...what?"

"Teach me how to seduce my Mr. Right."

"If I wanted to, which I don't, I could. But I won't."

Cat leaned back and smiled. "Bet you can't."

10

THIS REQUIRED SOME serious mental gymnastics, Luke decided, lying on the sofa in the dark. The new wrinkle had been added three days ago. For a while there the temptation she offered was almost more than a man could take. He'd managed to control himself. Barely. Right now he was waiting for Cat to come home from another date.

A date. How delightful for her.

Thanks to her, Luke hadn't had a decent date in weeks. His love life had gone to hell. He was permanently erect and would go into the *Guinness Book of Records* for the man with the hardest permanent erection in history. Probably for taking the most cold showers per day, too.

Mr. Right.

How could she have found this guy so fast? What did this jerk have that was special enough for her to abandon her lifelong dream of marriage?

And could Luke be chivalrous enough to put his own needs and desires aside if Cat truly had found her Mr. Right? Just the thought of Cat belonging to—

Chauvinist. A woman didn't *belong* to a man. Well, whatever the hell the term was, Luke didn't want Cat doing it with anyone. Not ever.

He rolled over, dragging the sheet under him into a

tangled mess. It was hot again. The door to the balcony stood wide open, a fan belligerently moving hot air around. He'd taken another icy shower. No surprise—it didn't help.

He was wearing the bare minimum—cotton briefs, in deference to Cat. Who wasn't even home. He wished he could at least discuss this with Nick. But Nick was unusually quiet these days. Suspiciously quiet, now that Luke came to think of it.

He punched his hot pillow, then jerked upright, only too pleased to be off the sticky leather sofa as he paced, building up a nice head of steam. He strode into the kitchen and turned on the light. He'd bake bread. He loved to cook. The combination of science and creativity, of tossing raw ingredients into a pot and turning out something edible, fascinated him. But bread making got rid of aggression. The pounding, pummeling and squeezing appealed to him, especially tonight.

He found his favorite mixing bowl, added all the ingredients and started kneading the dough by hand. Pounding his fists into the dough was marginally satisfying. Not as satisfying as making love to Cat. But right now, that wasn't an option.

And who had she gone out with tonight, anyway? Pummel. Had she said? Pummel. Was it Ted? Allan? Was it Nick again? Pummel, pummel, pummel. Who was Mr. Right? It was just like Cat to throw him off the scent like this.

She was doing the dating merry-go-round. Ted. Allan, Bob. Nick. Couldn't she see they were all players.

Luke greased the bowl and left the abused dough to rise under a clean cloth. How did she think he could go to work when he had to stay up till all hours of the night waiting up for her? The fact that it was only a little after nine and his usual bedtime was around eleven had no bearing on the matter.

An image of seventeen-year-old Cat flashed through his mind. That damned birthday. He'd known she'd gone out with friends. Through the kitchen window he'd watched her return, dancing her way across the lawn in the moonlight, looking like some delicate woodland nymph. The soft, floaty material of her dress had outlined her bare legs and snugly cupped her breasts. He'd been terrified down to his toes at the immediacy of his body's reaction. It had been the entire reason he'd kept his distance in the previous year. He'd been afraid of the magnetic draw she'd always had for him, the pull he'd thus far managed to resist.

He remembered vividly thinking, *Run. Escape before she comes inside.*

Instead he'd stood there in his dad's empty house, heart racing, anticipation churning in his gut. Knowing he had only seconds to make a clean getaway.

Knowing he'd wanted one taste before he died.

And he would die if his father ever caught him with his hands on her. The little sister he'd promised to protect. The defenseless semiorphan he and Dad had vowed would never be hurt again.

The back door had crashed open, and there she'd stood, swaying in the open doorway.

"Luke, you came." She'd sounded so delighted. Her exuberance had been contagious. He'd risen, hard and ready, to the occasion, and had known right then and there that he was damned.

One moment there'd been a safe, respectable ten feet of linoleum between them, the next instant Cat had flung herself into his arms, clinging like a baby monkey.

His embrace had been as far from brotherly as sugar from salt. Giving her no chance to voice a protest, he'd crushed his mouth down on hers. She'd tasted intoxicatingly sweet as her pliant body wrapped around his in the most compelling, amazing way, pressing her firm young breasts against his chest.

In the eleven years he'd known her, Cat had always been reserved, always trying to remain inconspicuous. Her exuberance that night had been totally unlike her.

He hadn't thought. He'd felt. With more passion than finesse, he'd pressed her supple young body against the refrigerator. He'd kissed her until they'd both been breathless, then he'd kissed her some more. He'd touched her breast through the flimsy fabric of her dress and wanted it all. Wanted her naked beneath him. Wanted her strong runner's legs wrapped about his waist. Wanted to sink into her wet heat and have his wicked way with her.

Finally it had penetrated his brainless state that Cat was struggling in his arms.

He felt the deep scalding flush of shame now, nine years later, as violently as he had then. There'd been no excuse for his behavior. Unless being a twenty-four-year-old with a sporadic love life and a suddenly enormously high sex drive counted.

Horrified at his loss of control, he'd let her go immediately. But not immediately enough to prevent her from throwing up on his shoes.

His horror at his own inappropriate conduct had manifested itself in a scathing lecture on *her* behavior.

With one wounded look, after his betrayal, Cat had fled.

He'd gone back the next day to apologize. Cat had been her usual quiet, contained, cheerful, kid sister self. Luke had been so relieved he'd almost kissed her in gratitude. Well, he was a slow learner.

He did the decent, honorable thing. He'd left her alone, and done everything in his power to reinforce their brother-sister relationship. It had worked out just damn well fine. Until now.

He wondered if they needed architects in China.

"YUM, IT SMELLS TERRIFIC in here. Been baking?" Catherine tossed her purse on the counter and eyed Luke's apparel. She rubbed her itchy elbow and grinned. He wore a navy-and-white-striped bib apron, and from the look of him, little else. "Interesting new fashion statement, even for you."

"It's hot in here."

"No kidding." Even with her hair piled up on top of her head and minimal clothing, she was hot. Looking at an almost naked Luke made her hotter still. She made a rapid inventory of the kitchen instead. Dirty dishes were piled haphazardly in the sink, and the doughy hooks from the Cuisinart lay on the flour-dusted counter.

She frowned. "What's wrong?"

"Nothing. Why?"

"You bake when you're uptight."

"I bake when I want to eat whatever I'm baking."

Right. "Okay. Is that bread ready?"

Luke shoved the dish towel-covered board across the granite center island. "Help yourself." He uncovered the loaf and snagged the butter dish before whacking off a thick, fragrant, yeasty slice. "Nice evening?" He leaned against the counter, arms folded, ankles crossed.

Catherine slathered butter on the hot bread and took a bite. "Mmm. This is fabulous. It was...terrific." Luke had terrific legs. Hairy, tanned, muscular. Runner's legs. Although he never ran when he could walk, or walked when he could be prone. She couldn't wait to get him prone. "What brought on this spurt of domesticity?"

"I have someone else I want you to meet," he said at the same time. "His name is Steve Manfield."

Catherine reached over her shoulder to scratch an itch between her shoulder blades. "Good grief! I told you, I've already found my Mr.—"

"Please tell me Mr. Right isn't Ted?"

"Nope. Not Ted," Catherine said obediently, and resisted rolling her eyes.

"Well, you should meet Steve before you decide. He's a decent guy. Owns his own insurance agency here in the city. Financially solid. Has a terrific house with a pool, which is appreciating in value everyday. Loves kids. Has a couple of dogs. I think you and old Steve will have a lot in common."

"With that glowing testimonial, how can a girl refuse?" Catherine said dryly. "I do, however. Refuse, that is."

"One date couldn't hurt, Cat. Just to be sure."

"I'm sure now."

"We'll double-date this weekend, how's that?"

Catherine shook her head in exasperation. She was sorely tempted to whack him over the head with the breadboard.

"Overkill, Luke. And a total waste of time. Besides, we're going to a wedding. Remember?"

Luke groaned. "I was trying to forge... Why are you scratching like that?"

"Don't ask." She considered squeezing between Luke and the opposite counter to get to the refrigerator and a glass of icy-cold milk. She'd hate to pass up any opportunity to touch him. Especially dressed the way he was right now. A nice slow shimmy, Catherine decided.

Luke waited until she was almost through the straits before he snagged her arm. His eyes did a rapid scan of her arms and shoulders, bared by the pumpkin-colored halter dress. "Are you aware you're covered with a red rash?"

"As a matter of fact, yes."

"Shellfish?"

Catherine rubbed her upper chest, where the welts were now on fire. "Would you pour me a glass of milk, please? I think there was some sort of lobster base in the sauce we had at the restaurant." The little container of crab she couldn't resist at Fisherman's Wharf before going into the movie alone had been worth a little itching.

He took down a glass, filled it and handed it to her. "Here. You ate it anyway." He shook his head. "Stay right there, I'll get the calamine."

Luke brushed past her to go to the cabinet where he kept his vast array of first-aid supplies—a five-year-old box of Band-Aids, a two-year-old bottle of aspirin and the calamine lotion. Luke was, as they said, always in rude good health. It warmed her heart to know he had the lotion, which only she used.

Catherine sipped the milk without tasting it. He had the neatest, tightest little butt she'd ever seen. Luke in underwear and an apron was the sexiest thing she'd ever seen in her life. More than her skin itched. Catherine bit her lip. What did she have to do? Use Nick's two-by-four over his head? Strip naked and lie on the floor at his feet?

Luke grabbed the paper towels from under the sink and came back with the pink bottle in his hand. "Turn 'round."

The first dab was nice and cold. His stiff cotton apron brushed the back of her legs as he stepped closer.

"What are you doing?" he asked, dabbing away at her shoulders with the calamine-soaked paper towel.

"Undoing the halter so you can get to my neck."

"Stop scratching."

"I'm rubbing."

"Don't do that, either." He pushed her hand gently out of his way, then his fingers touched her shoulder as he patted downward. She felt the warmth of his breath against her skin. It made the loose curls at her nape dance and tickle her neck. Moisture prickled between her breasts and she held her hand there to keep the top of the dress up, and her heart from jerking right out of her chest.

What she'd rather do was let go and turn around. She almost clucked, she was so chicken. Her breath jammed in her lungs. She stayed as she was, back turned, and let him dot and dab at the rash.

She felt like she had when she'd been a kid, standing on the highest diving board at the YWCA, her toes clenched around the end of the board, looking down at that pale blue water shimmering a mile beneath her. Wanting to jump, but sick with the adrenaline rush, breathless with excitement, dizzy with terror. One. Two. Three... She removed her hand and let her dress drop to her waist.

"What are you doing?" Luke demanded, voice hoarse. He stood directly behind her. When he breathed in, the fragrance of her skin blotted out all rational thought. When he breathed out, corkscrew tendrils of her upswept hair fluttered against her bare back. With a silent curse, he gritted his teeth and tried to ignore the unconscious invitation of a topless Catherine Harris. And he only had a view of her slender back peppered with cinnamon freckles, nasty pink blotches and smears of lotion. He didn't have to see her breasts to know she was naked from the waist up. Blood rushed from his head to his groin.

"Unless you're going to doctor all of me, I'll do my front while you do the back," Cat murmured, open palm extended over her bare shoulder. "Hand me the lotion, will you?"

For half a heartbeat their eyes met. Her lashes flickered as she gazed at his mouth for a fraction of a second. Her pupils dilated just a little as she looked up, directly into his eyes.

Heat sheeted Luke's body in a lightning-flash rush. God almighty, Cat had no idea what those amber eyes of hers could do to a man. He knew if he inspected himself he'd find the damned apron tented over his erection. He couldn't look anywhere other than into Cat's eyes.

So near and yet so far.

He wanted her so badly. But he knew if he touched her it would just make the wanting, the needing, the ache, worse. Not only would he have betrayed her trust, if he touched her like a lover, even once, he knew he'd never stop. And he'd never get over her.

It would be an irrevocable step.

One he would never take. But it was killing him.

Wordlessly he handed her the bottle of lotion. She half turned to reach for it, and he had a brief glimpse of the narrow span of her rib cage and one pale, perfect plump breast. His eyes shot back to her face. She seemed oblivious, and he dragged in another breath, drenched with the scent of her.

His physical reaction to her was bad enough to deal with. But this was day-and-night different. An odd feeling expanded through him. A feeling that had nothing to do with his rampant sexual desire for her. It felt unbearably sweet. Poignant. Sinfully rich. His heart hitched, and yearning filled his soul....

Then he saw himself in her eyes. And what he saw was security. Safety. Trust. Promises made. Vows kept. The thought worked as effectively as a bucket of ice water.

Almost.

Torture. And bless her sweet naive heart, she had no

idea. She believed she was safe with him. He let out a breath and tried to distract himself. Unfortunately, he still had her rash to contend with. He had to stand close, had to touch, had to breathe. He had to get laid. And soon. He was hanging on by the last sliver of his fingernails.

She trusts me. He dabbed all the way down to the slender span of her waist, making sure only the paper towel touched her smooth skin. "Can you do the rest yourself?" he asked, his tongue sticking to the dry roof of his mouth. He'd go directly to heaven for his restraint, and straight to hell for his thoughts. "Or do you need me to—"

She reached back and tugged at the short zipper at the small of her back. The sides flopped back, revealing the sweet curve of her waist, the gentle swell of her bottom and the beginning of cleavage. He went icy hot.

"Jesus. Did you go out tonight buck naked under this dress?" Luke croaked.

"Oh, good." She sounded relieved. "No line. I have on a thong," she told him mildly. "Feels like there's a whole bunch of itchies, right here." She brushed the pale flesh below her waist—well below her waist—with her thumb, while trying to look over her shoulder. "Can you see them?"

Luke prayed for an earthquake. A flood. A famine. A natural disaster. Something. Anything.

"Luke?"

He dabbed.

She moaned as the cold liquid soothed the burning itches.

He silently cursed. "That should do it, right?" His

voice was almost nonexistent, and as hopeful as that of a penitent.

With both hands, she started slithering the fabric of her dress up her thighs. "If you'd just do the back of my le—" She broke off and allowed the material to fall down to cover her legs again. "Never mind."

Thank God. He couldn't take any more.

She rubbed the end of her nose with the back of her hand. "I can do the rest, thanks."

"Did something happen tonight with—who was it?" Luke demanded.

Cat sighed, put the bottle down on the counter, then used both hands to retie the straps of her dress around her neck. She turned to face him. "Nothing happened with tonight's date," she snapped. "He is not the problem."

Luke touched her warm cheek. Longing rushed through him. He yearned to have the freedom to express all the emotions churning in his gut. He felt like an insensitive jerk. Something was wrong. He let his gaze move slowly over her tight features while she glared up at him. He dropped his hand, didn't know what to do with it, and folded his arms across his chest. She was utterly unaware of how she tied him in knots, and he'd better well keep it that way. He leaned back against the fridge, cocked his knee enough to mask the bulge in the apron, and tried his best to look... unhorny.

"Then tell me what the problem is, Catwoman. And I'll fix it for you."

"My Mr. Right doesn't even know I exist." She

glared at him as if it were his fault. "What can you to do about that, Luke Van Buren?"

Needing something to do with his hands, he pulled a clean mixing bowl out of the cabinet and placed it carefully on the counter between them. He looked at her. "What would you like me to do? Say the word," he said, gathering ingredients from shelves and refrigerator. He dumped everything haphazardly on the counter beside the bowl. "You know I'd do anything for you."

"How about if you stop moving around at the speed of light and listen, then?"

Luke leaned one shoulder against the fridge. He crossed his arms. "You have to say something, Cat. Or do you want me to guess?"

"Right. Tell you. Yeah. Absolutely."

Luke's eyebrows rose. He waited as she hoisted herself up onto the counter. "I have a problem—"

"And you need my deft touch."

"Deft touch?" Catherine hooted, amused. "You're as clueless as he is, you turkey."

"He who?"

"Mr. Right."

Luke groaned.

She crossed her ankles and leaned back. The silky fabric of her dress slithered up her bare thighs.

"Okay, we can talk about me helping you. If you're absolutely posit— What are you doing?"

She gave him an innocent look. "You said not to scratch. I'm rubbing."

"You're stroking," Luke said in a choked voice.

Cat shrugged. "Whatever. It feels great. This itch is driving me nuts."

"Hell's bells, Cat. Your itch is driving *me* nuts. Stop that! Tell me what the problem is, and let's work on it. Cat?"

"I'm thinking here."

He clenched his teeth, pushed away from the fridge and took out his measuring cups and the big wooden spoon he liked to use for mixing. Without measuring, he tossed butter, then brown sugar into the copper bowl.

"Right. What do you think I should do? Just pull out all the stops and seduce him?"

Luke jerked away from his mixing as if he'd been catapulted across the kitchen. Sugar and butter went flying.

"Hell, no!" He raked his fingers through his hair, leaving glimmering speckles of sugar in the dark strands.

She put up her hands. "You don't have to shout. It was a simple question. You refused to help me by educating me on seduction. Now I'm on my own. The question is how do I make him desire me? Share your vast experience and tell me."

Luke stuck the spoon back in the bowl and stirred it to China. "What's wrong with this Mr. Right of yours?" He broke eggs into the mixture as though he were doing intricate brain surgery.

She laughed. "Look, I know he likes me, but I want him to realize that he could love me. Right now he thinks of me as more of a—a friend."

"What's wrong with that?" Luke demanded. "That's a good place to start. Most couples start with less."

"Fine. Great. Terrific. But I'd like it to move a little faster than another twenty years of friendship."

Something in her tone made him stare at her with added intensity. *Nick. She's talking about Nick.* Luke's knuckles went white around the spoon. He stood very still. "How do you feel about this guy, Cat? For real."

Their eyes locked, and Cat said very quietly, "I love him with all my heart."

11

"YOU'RE IN LOVE WITH HIM?"

"Yes. Very much."

"The real thing?" Very carefully, Luke put the dough-covered spoon down on the edge of the counter and didn't notice when it clattered to the floor. This was Cat. Cautious, crablike Cat. He stared at her as if she were an alien life force. "Are you sure?"

"Without a shadow of a doubt."

For several seconds he searched her face without saying anything, then sighed and said heavily, "I have a sinking feeling I know who it is."

She shot him a glance. "You do?"

"Nick."

"Nick? Who said anythi—"

"Dammit, Cat. That's exactly what I thought." His voice rose to new heights. "He's a player, for God's sake. A *player*." Luke slammed his fist on the counter. Unfortunately, his hand hit the egg carton. The carton crumpled with a crackle as eggs broke.

Cat tilted her head to look at him. "Appearances can be deceiving," she said mildly. "Maybe he just hasn't met the woman right enough to make a commitment."

"My point exactly." Luke wiped his yolk-dripping fist on a paper towel.

"I believe with a little push, he'll realize he's a little in love with me already."

"A push off a high cliff without a safety net is more like it," Luke said grimly. *Not Nick*, he thought, his gut twisting.

This was his worst-case scenario. It was one thing for Luke to think it was Nick. But to have her confirm it...

The earthquake had come. The famine. The plague and the pestilence. She was in love with someone.

"Hey!" Cat socked him on the arm. "Are you in a coma, or what?"

"You deserve to have some sort of commitment. Jeez, Cat. I said I'd help you, and I will." *Even if it kills me.*

"By doing what exactly?"

Yeah. What? "Make him jealous?"

Cat gave him an odd look. "Make him...jealous?"

"You want to at least have some sort of declaration of commitment from Mr. Right, right? You know how competitive we are. One little hint that I'm interested in you, and Nick will charter a flight to Las Vegas before we've finalized the bet. Are you game?"

For several seconds she was apparently too stunned to speak. She closed her eyes and rubbed her hand across her forehead. "Sure." She smiled. "Why not?"

That seemed to have worked, Luke thought, relieved. "It's late. Why don't you go off to bed? I'm going to finish these cookies, and think about how we can execute Operation Mr. Right."

Execute being the operative word here.

LUKE'S THROAT CLOSED UP until he couldn't breathe. His chest felt as though an overweight elephant squatted directly on his heart. He realized that every time Cat had mentioned Mr. Right he'd felt physical pain. Agonizing pain. Pound your head on the wall pain. Rip your guts out pain.

He was going to give her a list of Nick's faults. There were a hundred things wrong with Nick. A million things—

Argh! There was nothing wrong with Nick, Luke admitted reluctantly. He and Nick had been best friends for most of their lives. Nick Stratton was honest. Honorable. Decent. And if Cat wanted him, it was Luke's sworn duty to make sure he protected her until Nick declared himself.

Oh, hell. Just the thought of Nick's hands anywhere on Cat's body made Luke's blood pound like a runaway train through his brain. His teeth ground together until his jaw ached. He wondered where he could dispose of the body.

But then he'd have to comfort her.

And if it wasn't Nick, then it would be someone else.

Luke couldn't leave a trail of bodies across the San Francisco Bay Area just because...just because he didn't want her hurt.

He could've helped her with anyone else.... *Liar!* Luke admitted roughly.

THE NEXT MORNING Luke casually strolled into his partner's office in the north turret carrying two cups of latte. Nick, dressed in a lightweight charcoal wool suit, tie in place, shoes polished, sat with his feet on his desk, staring out the window.

Luke, wearing jeans and a T-shirt, because he was going on-site, took a seat in the visitor's chair opposite the wide mahogany desk. "That's my favorite pose, Stratton."

Nick turned his head away from the city view and grinned. "Hey, old son, what's up? Thanks." He took the cup and popped the plastic lid. "To what do I owe the dubious honor of your presence at nine o'clock on a Wednesday morning?"

"A man can't bring his partner a cup of coffee?"

"Depends on what the man's up to." Eyes suspicious, Nick took a sip.

"I wanted to talk to you about Cat. Catherine."

"Catherine?" Nick frowned. "Why? What's wrong?"

"Nothing's wrong." *Damn*, Luke thought, this could prove to be awkward as hell. "How do you feel about her, Nick?"

Nick leaned back comfortably in his big leather chair. "Are you kidding? I'm mad about her."

"Seriously mad about her? Or mad about her for the next five minutes, like the rest of your harem?"

"And the answer to this question is important to you why?"

"Just answer the question."

"She's beautiful. Sexy. Smart... Hell, I'm halfway in love with her. Why?"

"Halfway in love with her?" Luke scoffed. "Get real. Since you obviously can't even commit to how you feel about her, I'm following up on your suggestion and taking her out myself."

Nick frowned and removed his feet from the desktop with a thud. He set his coffee down. "You and Catherine?"

"Yeah. Why not?"

"You mean like a date kinda thing?"

Nick *was* jealous. "Got a problem with that?" Luke demanded, revving up his belligerence for Cat's sake.

"But she's your sister."

"As you've told me so often, Cat's not my sister. All I'm doing is telling you my intentions."

"I see. And what are your intentions toward Catherine?"

"Honorable." Luke watched his friend's face.

Something flickered briefly in Nick's eyes before he expertly masked it. "Yeah?"

"Yeah!"

Nick took another sip of his latte. "I don't think so."

"What?"

"I said, I don't think so," Nick repeated coolly. "You told me weeks ago that you considered Catherine the next best thing to a doorstop. A sexless...sister. Now you're trying to tell me you want her? Give me a break. Wanna bet you want her because you know *I* want her?"

"No. This is not a betting situation."

"Why not? Everything's grounds for a bet."

"Not Catherine," Luke said seriously. The latte tasted like sweat socks. "Tell me, Nick. What do you see when you look at Cat?"

"A beautiful, sexy, desirable woman."

"That's my point. Cat is more than that. Much more. She's funny and wise, vulnerable and incredibly strong. She's...dimensional."

"Are you standing there telling me *you're* in love with her?" Nick asked incredulously.

"I'm taking Cat to Arizona for the weekend," Luke told him tightly, trying to remind himself that this was a strategy to help Cat.

Nick looked startled. "What?"

"Yeah. Wanna make something of it?"

"Are you in love with her?"

Admission ready to spill from his lips, Luke bit his tongue. Once spoken, the words would be out there in the atmosphere forever. Waiting to haunt and torment him for the rest of his miserable life.

God help him. He didn't just *want* Cat. He loved her.

"Are you?" Luke countered.

"Face it," Nick said. "We both have the hots for her. Vastly different emotions, old son. Vastly. Unfortunately, we both feel guilty as hell because we're so protective of her. Which is why I've held back. I've just been biding my time. We've watched her grow up, we've watched her bloom." He waggled his dark eyebrows. "And bloomed very nicely, too. But that's lust, pal. Just lust. Now the question is, which one of us will—"

"Don't say it." Luke stood up and glared at his ex-best friend. "Don't even think it, Stratton. Cat's off-limits to you from now on."

The pseudoanger was a nice touch. Unfortunately, his heart was racing and his eyeballs felt like they were about to pop right out of his head. *This is just an act*, Luke reminded himself, as he tried to unfurl his tightly clenched fists, to no avail.

"Keep away from her unless you're planning a wedding," Luke growled.

Nick almost fell off his chair. "A wedding? A wedding as in here comes the bride? Are you nuts! What about The Bet?"

"So winning The Bet is more important to you than Cat?"

"I didn't say that. Did you?"

"Maybe."

Nick leaned back, cupped the back of his head with his hands and swung his big feet up on top of his desk again. "Well, maybe from me, too."

"Make up your mind, Nick."

"Ditto."

They glared at each other.

THEIR FLIGHT TO ARIZONA was uneventful, if one discounted their close proximity on the plane. It was late evening by the time they arrived at the resort hotel. Luke had been lucky to get a room on the same floor as hers at such short notice.

Accompanied by the steamy smells of soap and bleach, Cat's room had a view of the back of the laundry room. No scenic overlook of Camelback Mountain, nor the pool, for Faith's only child.

"Mine's not much better. But I can have them move you if you like." Sitting on the foot of her bed, Luke tried to read her expression as she picked up various objects, fiddled with them, then put them down again. The soft fabric of her lavender dress clung to her legs and hips as she paced. Between the X straps on her back, her skin was creamy and lightly freckled in the lamplight. His mouth watered.

She'd been unusually quiet during the flight to Arizona, even more subdued when they'd arrived at the hotel where her mother's wedding was to be held the next evening.

"Nah, I don't need to change rooms. No big. It's only two nights. Besides, I didn't come for the view."

"Just the spectacle?"

Cat picked up the leather-bound room service menu and smiled slightly. "She does her best to outdo herself every time, doesn't she? No doubt this one will beat them all."

She flipped the laminated pages. "If I ever get married I'll combine all of Faith's most outrageous weddings into one huge blowout. Pull out all the stops. Go for broke." The menu plopped back onto the desk with the finality of a divorce decree. "Except for the elephant. That wasn't one of her better ideas."

"Yeah, elephant poop must've been hell on the laundry bill." *When I get married...* The words hit him like a fist in the gut. "You planning on getting married in the near future?" he asked casually.

She gave him an indecipherable look. "Let's get something to eat before I start gnawing on the fruit in that painting. Come on, Van Buren, get the lead out, I'm famished."

Was she missing Nick? Luke already felt like a pulled-taut rubber band, whitened by the excessive stretch. Any second now he was going to go *sproing*. He was sitting on a giant, king-size bed. Sheets turned back. Chocolate on the pillow. Lights turned low. He wouldn't need anything sweeter than Cat beside him.

Ain't gonna happen, pal. "One would think the guy was terminally dense not to fall over his feet getting to you," he offered casually.

Her lips twitched. "One would think. Do you want to hit the restaurants, or should we get room service?"

She'd been only mildly attentive when he'd told her about his conversation with Nick. Women were like that. Not interested until the knights drew blood. It had been damn close.

"Let's go out and eat, then reconnoiter. If you're not too tired, that is?" He felt too vulnerable right now to be anywhere near a horizontal surface with Cat in the same room. Surreptitiously, Luke glanced at the phone on the desk. No red light blinked, indicating Nick had called. Or Faith, for that matter.

It was 9:00 p.m. The wedding was set for six the next evening. Surely Faith could manage to squeeze in a few moments to see Cat? She hadn't seen her daughter in two years. No loss, as far as he was concerned. Cat picked up her purse just as there was a knock at the door. Their eyes met.

"I'll get it." Only too happy for a diversion, Luke opened the door. Faith What'sit-What'sit-What'sit stood out in the hall, wearing a white silk pantsuit with gold buttons and looking as though she'd stepped from the pages of *Vogue*. For a split second, Luke saw what his father had seen. The flawless complexion. The petite, yet curvy body. The incredible honey-red sweep of her hair. But unlike his father, Luke had always had twenty-twenty where Faith was concerned. She was high maintenance, low return.

He stepped back, opening the door wider. "Howdy, Stepmama."

She did a slight double take. "My goodness, Lucas. What a lovely surprise." She reached up to peck the air an inch from his cheek, then handed him the black silk garment bag she carried. "Put this somewhere, darling. Now, where's my baby?"

"Hi, Mother."

Faith came toward her, hands outstretched. "Let me look at you. Oh dear, I always forget what a big girl you are."

Their hands met briefly, her mother's cool and dry, Catherine's damp. She resisted wiping her palms on her dress. As always, in Faith's presence she felt gangly and plain and as though she took up too much space. She despised her own reaction to this beautiful stranger who was her mother. Faith was a softer, paler, more petite version of her offspring.

Smoky eyes skimmed Catherine from head to toe, swiftly and expertly cataloging to the last cent what each item of clothing had cost.

"My goodness, Catherine, are you still shopping at those dreadful discount stores? And those high heels not only make you simply tower over everyone, they make your feet look enormous."

"She doesn't tower over me." Luke came up behind Catherine and slipped his arm around her waist. "I think Cat has the sexiest feet since Cleopatra. And the only people she towers over are people too short to appreciate her height. With her impeccable taste, she could shop at the flea market and still look gorgeous."

His hand felt warm and solid on her middle. So did his defense of her. *Bliss.*

"How sweet," Faith said with a vague smile. "You always were her champion, weren't you, Lucas? Catherine, I only stopped by to drop off your gown for tomorrow. I've made an appointment for your hair at 9:00 a.m. Now that I see it's just as unruly as ever, I'll have Milo straighten it a little after he cuts it."

"She's not cutting one inch off her hair," Luke said flatly. He looked down at her, his arm still around her waist. "Are you, Cat?"

"Nope." Her mother would have given the hairdresser strict instructions, Catherine knew. She'd been caught unprepared only once. Then she'd found herself with an oddly avant-garde asymmetrical do that made her feel like a lopsided Little Orphan Annie until it grew out. There was no use arguing with her mother now. Catherine would cancel the appointment tomorrow.

"How are you, Mother? Where's the lucky groom?"

"You know it's bad luck for him to see the bride before the wedding. Chandler is staying with a friend until tomorrow." Faith craned her neck at her much taller daughter. "And I think that now we're both adults, you should call me Faith, don't you, darling?" She smiled, showing straight, beautifully bleached white teeth. Husband number five had been a dentist. "We can pretend we're sisters. Won't that be fun?"

Great, Catherine thought wryly, *everyone wants me to be their darn sister.*

This was the first time in living memory that her mother's darts completely missed their mark. Startled by the realization, Catherine knew she was seeing Faith through Luke's eyes. It was a revelation.

Like a cartoon character with a lightbulb blinking overhead, she saw her mother as a sad, lonely woman who filled her life with loveless marriages and buying sprees because she couldn't bear to spend a moment alone. The fact that Faith was a petty, selfish woman filled with her own self-importance had nothing to do with who Catherine was. The knowledge came as a shock. For years she'd felt as useless and unattractive as her mother told her she was. Faith's perception was not reality.

"Something to drink, Faith?" Luke asked, still glued to Catherine's side. She was grateful for his strength. Both his arm and the moral support he provided. However she tried to rationalize, she always felt battered around her mother. "Eye of newt, perhaps?" he added.

"No, thank you, darling. I have to run. I'm having a massage in a little while. I just wanted to give Catherine her gown." She glanced around to see where Luke had put it. "Do come and look. I bought it for you in Paris, darling." She eyed her daughter the only way Catherine had ever seen her mother look at her. Critically.

"Although now I look at you it might be just a teeny bit snug around the hips. You have packed on a little weight, haven't you? And my Lord, what have you been doing to your poor skin? Must you persist on going out in the sun and getting all freckled? Darling, I insist you use that cream I sent you."

"Isn't Cat lucky you're marrying a plastic surgeon?" Luke interjected mildly, his hand tightening fractionally on Catherine's hip. "Not that she'd ever need it. But if she does, in thirty or so years when she's your age, she can also have her face extensively excavated and remodeled free. Of course, by then you'll probably be married to a mortician. Easy come, easy go."

Catherine almost choked. She couldn't look at Luke in case she started to laugh.

"Gracious, Luke. You know I was only sixteen when I had Catherine. I was practically a baby myself."

Faith had slipped up and gotten pregnant at twenty-nine, not sixteen. But for as long as she could remember, Catherine had been blamed for the inconvenience. Her beautiful mother couldn't frown anymore, she noticed. Faith must have had those Botox shots to kill the nerves in her face. It was rather odd to see the expression in her mother's eyes but not see the wrinkled brow that should have accompanied it.

Faith pulled the garment bag away and held up the dress. If nothing else, her mother had impeccable taste. The gown was a slim, floor-length column of flame colored silk. There was no embellishment whatsoever, just flowing fiery silk jersey, expertly cut on the bias.

"Interesting color choice for a wedding," Luke observed blandly. "Wouldn't black have been more appropriate?"

"Black is no longer *très élégant*." Faith tilted her head as she held the dress up in front of Catherine. She eyed what was certainly a one-of-a-kind designer gown with a small pout. "I thought the color would be quite striking with Catherine's coloring, but now..."

Not in a trillion years, Catherine thought without hostility. There was no way on God's green earth her mother had ever thought this color would flatter her.

"You were absolutely correct," Luke said with mock admiration. "This will look dynamite on Cat. Admittedly, not everyone could pull off wearing this dramatic hue. For instance, it would completely drain all that hectic color right off your face, and make your hair look a little like straw, wouldn't it? It only works because of Cat's youth and beauty. And of course, the stunning deep color of her hair."

Catherine jabbed Luke in the ribs with her elbow. "How many people are coming to the wedding?" she asked quickly, before the giggle in her chest could burst free. To sober up, she imagined all the wedding guests staring at her butt in the skintight dress. She shuddered. Fortunately, she'd never see any of them again. Her mother never invited the same guests to two weddings in a row. Catherine was the unlucky exception.

"Only twelve hundred. Chandler wanted to keep it intimate, bless his heart."

Twelve hundred people staring at my rear. Oh joy. Catherine's eyes met Luke's. She saw the answering humor, and the question, *Are you all right?* She gave a small nod. A thousand-plus guests had not been invited a week ago, when Faith had called her daughter. Catherine gave a mental shrug. It wasn't important.

Faith recovered and handed the dress to her. "Well, I did my best. Just suck everything in for a couple of hours. It should be just fine. I must bid you au revoir. My masseuse awaits. Walk me to the door, darling."

Catherine wondered if Faith called everyone "darling" simply because she couldn't remember their names. Probably. She handed the dress to Luke and walked her mother to the door.

"Night, Faith," he called from across the room. "I'm looking forward to meeting old Chandler tomorrow. Hope we get a chance to chat. Dad filled me in on some of your more hilarious antics. I can't wait to share them with your next new...ah, *this* husband. We should have him rolling in the aisle."

Cat gently closed the door behind her speechless mother. She slid the bolt home, then turned to face him.

Cat had the oddest expression on her beautiful face. Oh, man. Was she going to cry?

"I'm sorry, Cat, I hate the way Cruella De Ville talks to you. Let's face it, your mother is a caricature—"

With a war whoop, Cat raced across the room and flung herself exuberantly into his arms. "My hero!"

Her mouth slanted down on his. Perfect synchronicity; his was right there to meet it. He hugged her close. Man, she felt incredible. She laughed against his mouth, and he'd never felt anything as intoxicating in his life.

"My dragon in shining armor." Her tongue curled around his with pure, unadulterated carnal intent.

His arms tightened around her. She kissed him and kissed him and kissed him. As though there was no tomorrow. He did the only thing he could: he kissed her back. Just for a minute. Just to slake his thirst. Just to quench his centuries-old desire for her. She tasted of the tears she hadn't shed while her mother was in the room. She tasted of joy. She tasted of yearning.

She tasted of heaven.

She tasted…off-limits.

He wasn't Mr. Right, and he'd better take a moment here to remind both of them.

As much as he wanted to go on kissing her forever, his hands automatically circled her waist to hold her at bay. There was only so much he could stand. He dragged his willing mouth away from the sweet succulence of hers. He hadn't resisted her for ten years to fail now. "Uh, Cat—"

Instead of answering, she gave him a little hip shove. They landed with a small thud on the bed behind him.

12

CAT PEPPERED PASSIONATE kisses on his mouth, his chin, his throat.

A blinding, dizzy hunger swamped him, so deep, so profound, he shook with it. Wrapping her more tightly in his arms, he feasted on the softness of her lips, on the slick duelling of her agile tongue, on the press of her slender body to his.

He tried to resist. He really did. He sent up a fervent prayer, but it was too late. Her breath feathered against his ear. How could she know there was a direct line from ear to groin? Panicked, he realized his body parts were disengaging from his brain. The brain that knew this was an incredibly dangerous situation.

The narcotic kiss went on and on. The alarm bells in his head became more distant as she arched against him. With unsteady hands, Luke tried to shift her off his body and out of temptation's way. Unfortunately, his hands seemed to be holding more than pushing.

Cat's eyes turned to liquid amber as she looked down, his name on her lips a shape without a sound. Then she dipped her head again.

He attempted to avoid her avid mouth. Her tongue was extremely sneaky. Her hips wriggled to get more comfortable, in the process hiking her dress up, baring more leg.

"What are you—doing?" he gasped, as her hand stroked down his side, evoking an intense shudder of desire. Her fantastic hair made a fragrant cave about their faces as she pulled the tail of his shirt from his jeans and kept him pinned to the bed with her body. Her eyes, so close they glittered like ancient amber, stared into his.

"Know something?" Her whisper, a hairsbreadth from his mouth, tethered him in place. Never in his life had he been so tempted. Found his need so great. Wanted a woman this much. And for so long. He had to battle the heat curling through him. For both of them. Yet the scent of her filled him to the brim. He...had to...think. Right. That was it. He had to think. With his brain.

She nibbled the corner of his mouth. "You talk too much." She clutched at his hair with one hand, the other busy tugging and ripping at his clothes.

A sensual fog clouded his reason. Her kisses were succulent. Rich with need. Delicious with desire. Her breath was warm against his lips, the inside of her mouth hot. Wet. Sweet. Hungry.

Having her like this felt so good it hurt. There wasn't a cell in Luke's body that didn't crave her like an addict. But he had to be sensible. His fingers curled around her upper arms to gently push her away.

Instead he found his hands sliding over the smooth skin of her shoulders in a caress. "You don't know what you're doing," he said desperately, his voice thick with hope and need.

"I'll get better with practice," Cat assured him, missing the point completely. Taking an ear in each hand, she held his head so he had to look at her. Her pupils appeared dark and enormous. "I'm a big girl, Luke. I know what I want."

She was curious, he forced himself to remember. Of course she was curious. His heartbeat kicked into a higher gear at the look of determination in her amber eyes. Luke groaned. She was long past the age where a woman took a lover. And he was the designated candidate. She considered him safe. She knew he'd do anything for her.

"No, wait. Cat—just—hold on a—"

She was a virgin. If he didn't have several really good reasons why he shouldn't proceed with this, that one would do it. He had to let her down gently. He was going to gently disentangle their bodies. Yes, he was. As soon as he came up with a reason that wouldn't hurt her. As soon as he could move, quiet his own raging hormones... As soon as his brain came back online.

"Uh, Cat? Why don't we talk about this?"

"Oh, Luke. You smell so good!"

A low, primal moan escaped him as she laved a warm, wet tongue over his right nipple. He forced himself not to react. But oh, God—he'd ached for this for weeks. Months. Years. Decades. He struggled for control.

And lost.

"Still sure?" he rasped.

"Please make love to me."

Her eyes lost focus as he bent his head and touched his mouth to hers. The kiss zinged through her bloodstream like potent alcohol. While he distracted her with the amazing versatility of his hot tongue in her mouth, Luke pulled the cotton knit dress down to uncover her breasts.

His eyes gleamed when he saw her strapless, lavender satin demi-bra. "Oh, man, touching you feels like a dream." He traced the pale swell above the cups, making her shiver.

"I'm real."

"Thank God. This looks incredible on you." His smile was feral. "It'll look even better on the floor."

His touch became almost reverent as his hand skimmed across her breasts. She arched upward, encouraging a firmer touch. But Luke wanted to explore. Lazily. Methodically. Catherine moaned as his thumbnail brushed her aroused nipple through the thin satin. While she desperately wanted the exquisite torture to last, her body demanded more immediate gratification.

"Luke..." She took his hand and pressed it hard against her. He found the front clasp of her bra. The cups fell away, baring her to his hot, damp breath. Luke palmed one breast at his own speed, his hand hot against her.

"Better than a dream." He dipped his head and, gentle as a butterfly, settled his lips on her nipple. It felt...exquisite. Then he sucked the hard nub deep into the cavern of his mouth, making her body arch with pleasure. A blinding shimmer of lust shot straight to her crotch. Mindless and frantic, Catherine clutched the back of his neck. Her need went beyond his gentle touches. She throbbed. She ached. She had to have...

"Luke...please..."

His lips closed with delicate greed over the other nipple. She didn't want delicate, she wanted desperate.

"Luke, take off m-my dre—" She swallowed. "Naked. I want to be na—ah!" Long moments ticked by before she remembered what she'd been trying to say.

"No rush," he said between nibbles and licks.

"Yes," she told the top of his head breathlessly as the pressure inside her built. "There is."

"No way am I going to rush through the hors d'oevres just because you're greedy for the main course. Relax, Catwoman, you're in good hands."

"Great hands," she assured him. "But *slow* hands."

Luke's chuckle vibrated through her chest. He cupped and kneaded the neglected breast while increasing suction on the other nipple. Driving her insane. Her head thrashed from side to side, her hips arched up off the bed as he blew on the wet bead. He bit down, not so gently, his fingers squeezing the twin with the same intensity. Then he skimmed her dress up her thighs. Catherine vaguely felt the air cool her bare legs. Luke's palm burned a path from knee to upper thigh.

"I..." Air spilled from her lungs as, with a low growl, he kissed her mouth, nibbling and teasing as his hand reached its goal.

...love you.

The feel of his fingers brushing the apex of her thighs through the thin fabric of her panties made her body writhe in response.

His finger dipped skillfully into the top elastic of her lavender satin panties. "Easy. Easy." Luke paused to breathe reassurances, then his mouth came down on hers once more.

Catherine felt her face grow warm as he intimately stroked her. She blushed hotter at the moisture his fingers encountered. While his clever mouth worked magic, Catherine shuddered, her entire body sensitized to Luke's touch. It was electrifying. Amazing.

He grazed the corner of her mouth. His lips traveled over her eyelids to close her eyes against the bright light. She felt the tips of his fingers brush satin-crushed curls, and she shivered deliciously. She moved her legs, aroused beyond bearing.

Luke deepened the kiss. His fingers sneaked into the slick wetness between her legs. He made a sound, almost of pain, as he slid a long finger deep inside the swollen folds. A low, hungry noise came from her own throat. Too much. It was too much. She shifted frantically against the scratchy hotel bedspread.

Luke lifted his head, his eyes dark and smoky. "Still with me?"

Catherine swallowed. Every nerve ending in her body screamed for the sweet release his fingers promised. "I think I've gone ahead," she murmured thickly as the scent of her own arousal mixed with the dark erotic fragrance of Luke's skin.

Dimly she heard him chant her name over and over again as he pressed her face against his hard, sweaty chest while aftershocks rippled through her.

God, she loved him. She loved the twist of his mouth as he concentrated on her pleasure. She loved how tender he was with her. How careful. She loved the deep bass of his voice, and the dark sexy taste of his mouth. She loved the smell of his skin and the silken texture of his hair. She loved having his fingers buried deep inside her.

Her choppy breath huffed. Luke's shuddered to a stop. Good. Suddenly shy, Catherine buried her face against the flat plane of his stomach. And inhaled the unique fragrance of an aroused Luke Van Buren. He smelled like her every fantasy. Her heart, already pounding, shifted into a primitive beat. Reflexively, her fingers tightened around him.

He growled low in his throat, then struggled to get something out of his back pocket and at the same time shimmy out of his jeans. She heard the double thud of his shoes hitting the carpet, the whoosh of his pants joining them on the floor.

"Wallet," he grunted, flipping it open to remove a foil packet. He ripped into it with his teeth, then handed her the rolled rubber.

Catherine stared at the tiny coil. What was Luke doing with a rubber in his wallet? He certainly hadn't been planning on sleeping with her on this trip.... Her heart thudded. *Don't go there*, she warned herself. *Don't even think about that*.

She looked from the condom to the bulge beneath his briefs. "You need kingsize, not this dinky sample! Oh, Luke—"

"It'll fit. Trust me. Here." He snatched it back. "I'll do it this time. I have only so much control left."

He sheathed himself, then groaned when he glanced up to see her avid attention focused on his hands. "If you stare at it like that I'm going to come before we even get started."

Catherine wished to God she could switch off her brain. *Tell me you love me. That'd help.*

He shot her a quick smile that twisted her heart. Then made quick work of the small satin triangle of her underwear, tossing the scrap of fabric aside. "Ah, Cat, so pretty."

With one knee, he nudged her legs farther apart and slid into the cradle of her thighs. The sensation of his hardness against the vulnerable portal of her body made Catherine tense.

"Relax, sweetheart."

Reflexively, her body stiffened. She bit her lip and tried to relax. *I love you. I love you....*

The fullness of his entry pinched as she opened to accommodate him. Tears sprang to her eyes and she hissed as her body tried to resist the tearing pain. Instinctively, her hips and knees tried to push him out and off.

Luke froze. "Cat?" He reared up to look at her face. "God, sweetheart, want me to stop?"

She tried to counteract her body's natural instinct, and wrapped her arms more tightly around him so he didn't roll away. This was Luke. Luke, the man she'd loved forever. Luke's fingers in her hair. Luke's breath mingling with hers. Luke's body intimately connected with hers. After what seemed like a lifetime of denial, they were on the same page at last. She wasn't going to ruin it now. "I'm—just hurry up and get it over with, okay?" *Hurry up and take my virginity and get back to the good part.*

The tendons in his neck stood out in sharp relief as he cupped her cheek in a tender hand. She felt him move inside her. "You're hating this," he stated. "Aren't you?"

"No!" He saw right through her. "Yes," she admitted reluctantly. White-lipped, he started to withdraw. Catherine squeezed her eyes shut and tightened her limbs around him.

"Finish." She couldn't look at him, she was so embarrassed.

He dropped his head and rested his forehead on hers. "I should have had the strength to tell you no."

Oh, God. Not again.

A sob vibrated deep in her chest. She wished with all her heart that she'd never made him do something he hadn't wanted to do.

"You've always given me what I wanted. Even when it's bad for me. Finish what I started, Luke. Then it'll be done."

Not once had he said he loved her. Not even a whisper of his feelings for her. What was the main event in her life, was, for Luke, a night of sex with an inept but willing partner. Catherine bit her lip. A fumbling, inexperienced, clumsy partner. Weighty sorrow settled like a lead blanket on her chest. *Don't let me cry. Please, don't let me cry.*

It wasn't Luke's fault that he didn't reciprocate her feelings. She couldn't make him love her. The earlier beauty of their lovemaking dissipated, a crying ache too big to ever be filled.

Deep inside, the old insecurity reared its ugly head. She was seventeen, seeing his face twisted with anger and regret just before he walked away from her. Now she felt the exact same bottomless ache of loss. The same bleak understanding that she was on her own. And always would be.

Just because Luke was making love to her didn't mean she had his heart. And without his heart, their lovemaking was a hollow victory. He was sorry she'd seduced him.

She'd taken the biggest gamble of her life.

And lost.

The wonderful feeling of euphoria was gone, but she held on to Luke as tightly as she could, wrapping him close with limbs and will as he pumped into her like a man possessed.

His muscles trembled as he tried to move more slowly within her. "O-kay?" he panted.

No. Her skin and her yearning felt too raw to tolerate his touch.

"Sure." She buried her face against his neck. She needed a dark room and time alone. She wanted to turn back the clocks to before she'd made monumentally wrong choices with the right man.

Catherine's heart ached unbearably, and tears leaked into her hair as she stroked the straining muscles of Luke's back while he had sex with her.

Iloveyouloveyouloveyou.

Stupidstupidstupid. What in God's name had he done? Still buried deep inside her, incapable of moving, Luke breathed in the scent of their lovemaking. A chill that had nothing to do with the air conditioner raced across his skin. She'd hated it. He'd known the second her body had tensed and she'd realized who was making love to her. Mr. Wrong.

He'd not only taken her precious virginity, but he'd taken it like a no-finesse pillaging Mongol.

"Luke, I lo—"

"Want the light off?" he asked at the same time, rolling away from her.

Silence pulsed, a living presence in the room. "Sure."

He carefully extricated himself from her, not touching more than he had to. She flinched and struggled to cover herself. The pale purple material of her dress was twisted around her middle. She tugged and pulled at it, not looking at him.

God. He'd never seen a more abject picture of embarrassment in his life. He pulled the edge of the sheet to cover her pale, perfect, freckled body. "You're not going to be sick, are you?"

"No." Her voice was muffled by the arm she'd flung over her eyes. The only way his little crab could hide.

He reached out and clicked the light off, plunging the room into darkness, then lay down beside her. Inches separated their bodies. Miles separated their needs.

"That was probably the dumbest thing I've ever done in my life," he said with a sigh. "I'm sorry, Cat."

The pause was so long he wondered if she'd fallen asleep. Down the corridor someone broke the thick silence, filling an ice bucket. The room smelled of sex and heat and lost opportunities. Beside him, Cat lay mute.

"Can you forgive me?" An overwhelming sense of dread settled on him.

"Of course."

"That's not how it's supposed to be done." He filled the excruciating silence with confessions. "And it was my fault. I should have realized that, without love, it would be harder for you to take. I just hope to God I haven't spoiled it for you with the next man."

"The next... You t-think—you think if it wasn't right with you it would possibly be right with someone else?" she asked bitterly into the darkness.

He reached out to touch her. She jerked away. God almighty. Luke pressed hard fingertips into his burning eye sockets. He should be shot.

"Trust me, sweetheart. Yes. Loving the person makes all the difference in the world."

"If you say so." A world of doubt colored her words.

"Are you really okay?"

"Couldn't be better."

"If I go get a warm, wet towel will you let me—"

"No!" She cleared her throat and repeated the word with less vehemence. "I'm going to get up in a minute and t-take a shower."

It was evident what she really wanted was to see the south end of his sorry ass heading north. Luke's elbow bumped her ribs as he rolled over. She flinched. He swore under his breath. Oh, Lord. How was he going to fix this? What could he say? What could he do?

Hands stacked under his head, and out of temptation's way, Luke stared up at the ceiling with an aching heart. Beside him, she shifted restlessly, embarrassed and uncomfortable with him now. He'd blown it and blown it bad. He wanted to slide his arm under her shoulders and pull her back into his arms and against his thundering heart. He wanted to be articulate.

Dammit. He wanted to be Mr. Right.

"You know this changes our relationship, Cat." It had to be said. Because he was trying so damn hard not to let any of the pent-up frustration and emotion seep out of his voice, it came out flat and surly.

"I don't want it to change," Cat said fiercely. She shifted; her leg brushed his. "Sorry."

"You don't want it to change?"

"No. I like things just the way they were before."

"You want to forget this ever happened?" His hand bumped her nose as he reached out to touch her.

"Ow. Yes."

"Sorry. Are you okay?"

"Sure. Hey, Van Buren, don't you have your own bed?"

"Are you crying?" he asked softly. *Yes, she's crying, you insensitive, lowlife moron.*

"Sinuses."

"Probably the air-conditioning." *Yeah, right.* "You kicking me out, Catwoman?"

"Don't take this personally, Luke, but you're taking up both halves of this bed, and I need to get some sleep before the main event tomorrow."

How much more personal could this get? Luke thought bitterly. He was completely naked. She had half her clothing on. He'd been so wild for her he hadn't even noticed. Of course she wasn't used to a man in her bed. Especially not Mr. Wrong. She'd been a virgin. Just because he'd never been any woman's first was no excuse.

"Can I at least wait until I get my breath back?" *Until*

I can think of something to say or do that will make this better for you?

"Hmm? Oh, sure. Gasp away." The mattress shifted. "I'm going to the bathroom. See you in the morning."

See you in the morning?

He heard her pad across the carpet. The bathroom door slammed shut. He watched for a sliver of light. He waited in vain.

Luke's throat closed. He was no Casanova, but he knew he had more finesse than this. What the hell was with him, anyway? He was so discombobulated with the taste, the touch, the smell of Cat that he didn't know up from down or in from out. Now, when he wanted to be smooth and suave and say the words she needed, wanted, deserved to hear, he'd fumbled badly. Even if he was Mr. Wrong, he should have made it good for her.

Not only had Cat lost her virginity to the wrong damn guy, he'd made her first sexual experience awful. He'd been a lousy lover. And if that wasn't enough, he'd betrayed her trust, broken his promises and hurt her in all the ways a man could.

Yeah. He was a real prince of a guy.

He wanted to love her all night. He wanted to love her forever. Instead he'd behaved like a sixteen-year-old with his first girl. Hell. He felt like a sixteen-year-old with his first girl. With startling clarity, Luke realized that the last few weeks with Cat had been foreplay. Blow-your-socks-off, let's-get-ready foreplay. He'd had about as much willpower as a wet rag.

Luke wiped his damp palms on the tangled sheets.

He felt as if he were traveling through an emotional storm. They'd taken an irrevocable step.

He wanted to howl like a savage beast. He wanted to burst into the bathroom, grab hold of her and toss her over his shoulder. He wanted to bring her back to this mangled bed and make love to her slowly, tenderly, until they were both too weak to move.

He wanted to grab her by her shoulders and demand she see that *he* was Mr. Right.

But Cat's feelings had to be paramount. Not his own. He knew Cat inside and out.

Luke jerked upright, eyes narrowed on the bathroom door.

He did a mental forehead slap. Damn right, he knew her inside and out.

No way would his Cat make love with a man she didn't love.

What had he been thinking?

As insecure as Cat was, she would never have slept with him if she didn't love him. The fool woman was trying to be noble and save him from himself.

Luke realized something else. He'd been so busy trying not to seduce her, he hadn't noticed that she'd been doing her damnedest to seduce *him* for weeks.

His heart took flight.

13

BLINDED BY TEARS, Catherine leaned her hip against the bathroom counter. The second she'd slammed the door behind her she'd yanked the dress, wound like a shroud around her middle, up and over her head. She was absolutely mortified.

It didn't help matters that she knew she was the one responsible for her own humiliation. *The idea was for Luke to make the first move, remember?* she castigated herself, while choking back a sob.

Didn't she have enough problems without this? One of the buttons on the back of the sundress had caught in her hair. She was stuck with her face covered, her arms pinned overhead by the inside-out dress, and no way to get free.

This would be funny. In about ninety-eight years.

The harder she struggled to free her hair, the tighter the tourniquet became around her upper arms. Furious, frustrated and trying to cry silently, she yanked savagely at the snarl behind her head. The harder she tried to free herself, the more fruitless it became. The harder she tried to be quiet, the more the sobs hurt her chest. The harder she tried not to love Luke, the more her heart ached.

"Damn. Damn. Damn."

The door snicked open. "Need help?"

Catherine shrieked, then said bitingly, "Dammit, Luke. I'm stark naked here!" It was pretty obvious she couldn't reach for a towel, let alone cover herself with her hands. She started to turn around, then quickly changed her mind. Besides, he'd seen every freckly inch of her already. "Get out, Van Buren!"

"Hmm. This looks *very* interesting."

What a particularly weird situation this was—standing here buck naked, arms immobilized over her head, blind, furious and humiliated. "Find me a pair of scissors, then leave."

"Hair caught?" Although he wasn't touching her, Catherine could feel the warmth of Luke's skin all down her left side. "Why don't you let me try to untangle it instead of cutting it?"

"Because," she said through her teeth "I don't want you anywhere near me. Go away."

There was absolutely no point in rehashing what was obviously a no-win situation. She loved him. He cared about her. Close, but no cigar. She'd get over loving him. At about the end of the next millennium, but by God, she could do it. Starting now when she felt the heat of his hand on her hip. She crowded against the cold porcelain sink.

"I don't want you to touch me," Catherine told him with as much dignity as she could muster.

"Darn," Luke said softly, picking her up in his arms like Rhett about to carry Scarlett up the stairs. He was naked. Why hadn't he dressed? "Isn't that too bad."

"Put me down. Dammit, Luke. I'm not joking, put me do—" He dropped her on the bed. Fresh tears sprang to her eyes, tears that had little to do with the fierce pull on her tangled hair.

"Don't suppose you had a chance to wash up yet?" Luke asked conversationally.

Catherine could feel his eyes traveling down her body, and was grateful for the dress covering her face as she blushed. She wiped her hot, wet cheek on her upper arm. "I hate you," she told him feelingly. "Go to your room."

She heard his departing chuckle. What...? Water ran. He was in the bathroom. Like a contortionist, she felt around the bottom of the bed with her toes for the sheet, hoping to cover herself before he came back.

"Amazing." The mattress depressed as he sat next to her. "Maybe you *should* have joined the circus."

"I won't be at your mercy forever, Lucas Van Buren. Don't!" she warned as he touched her thigh.

"Let me at least do this, Cat." His deep voice sounded achingly soft. "Please?"

The man was infuriating. "At least turn the light off."

The warm washcloth touched her intimately. Catherine almost shot off the bed.

"No."

She'd already forgotten the question... Oh, yes. The light. "What's this? The equivalent of a paper bag over my head?"

Luke laughed. "The equivalent of tying you to the bedpost."

"There are no bedposts."

"Exactly."

Catherine quivered like a horse at the starting gate as

he stroked her intimately with the rough terry cloth. The heat of her skin dried the tears on her cheeks. She'd never felt more vulnerable and exposed in her life, and it had nothing to do with being naked. Well, not much, anyway. How could he do this to her? Didn't he know what his earlier rejection had done to her?

Luke efficiently finished bathing her with the washcloth, then tossed the cloth aside. She felt him get off the bed.

"See you in the morning," she said briskly. *Not if I see you first.*

"Ah, my little crab. Convenient that you can hide under that pretty dress of yours. How lucky can a guy get?" The mattress between her feet depressed. She shrieked. She'd pictured him dragging on his pants and walking to the door.

He picked up her right foot. "Don't scream so loudly, Cat. It would be extremely embarrassing if hotel security burst in here and saw you like this. We'll start here."

Catherine's toes curled as his warm hand closed around her instep.

"The first time I fell in love with these feet was...oh, I guess you were about sixteen." His thumb caressed the length of her arch with sure, strong strokes. She tried to pull away, but he wouldn't let go. "You were sitting by the pool. You had on a swimsuit the same color as the water, do you remember? And you were painting your toenails Passion Pink. I thought you were the prettiest sight I'd ever seen."

"You're c-crazy. My feet are huge."

"Nah, your feet are just the right size." Moist breath flirted with her toes. She instinctively tried to tuck them out of sight. Luke chuckled. "Remember when we went shopping? Holy hell, Catwoman, I should be nominated for sainthood! I wanted to grab your feet, and...do...this...." He sucked her toes into the wet cavern of his mouth.

Catherine almost came off the bed. Dammit, she wanted to see...no, she didn't. She lay back against the mound of pillows and felt the slickness of his tongue as he ran it along the underside of her toes. The sensation was indescribable.

"Luke..." She had no idea what she wanted to say, so it was a good thing he ignored the interruption. He licked and sucked and nibbled her toes, instep, arch, heel. It was the most intimate of seductions, yet he'd gone no farther than her ankles.

By the time he set the second foot down on the bed, Catherine's heart raced and she felt as limp as an overcooked noodle, yet as wired as if she'd just run a marathon. Blinking open her eyes, she wished she could see Luke's face. But the darn dress was still firmly over her head.

"Luke, could you please—"

"Now I noticed your ankles a lot earlier, I must admit. You were probably fifteen or so. You'd just bought those gold high heels for that dorky Tony's prom, remember?" Luke's thumb caressed her right anklebone, while his lips skimmed over the left. The sensation shot to her very core. "You came down the stairs and the first thing I saw were your ankles. I about swallowed my tongue. World class ankles, these."

He paid homage to every indentation. How could licking her ankle be erotic?

"You were dating Anna Silk at the time." Catherine shifted on the bed. Wanting to...wanting. "I was spitting jealous of her, and all those other girls you brought home to introduce to Dad. They were always beautiful.... You don't remember Anna at all, do you?"

"No. I remember a young girl who was all wild red hair and witchy eyes. I remember wishing she'd hurry and grow up."

His tongue felt slippery and rough at the same time as he laved her anklebone.

"I loved you quite desperately when I was fifteen, you know."

His hands stroked up her calves. "Did you?" Luke whispered.

"Oh, yes..." Catherine's body vibrated like a tuning fork. "I'd loved you from the moment we met. But that was the year of my first full-fledged crush. You were so romantically wounded and brooding."

"Was I?"

She struggled anew with her recalcitrant hair and that darn button. "I must have driven you crazy trailing after you. You accused me of stalking you, remember?"

Luke kissed the back of her knee. His lips felt hot, and the touch of his mouth sent a shaft of pleasure skittering up her leg. "I wasn't very kind."

"No, you weren't. But I understood. You didn't sleep over at the house very often, but when you did I'd try to be with you at every opportunity. I was starting to feel very grown-up, and I couldn't understand why you didn't notice me."

"I noticed. As I recall, you came home from a barbecue and you were wearing those funky shorts that came down to here." The edge of his nail skimmed midknee. "Remember?"

Remember? She could barely think now. "You m-mocked me about those long shorts."

"Only to prevent myself from dropping to the ground and licking these knees. Trust me, Cat. I had dreams about these knees...." His tongue laved each knee in turn, while his clever hands stroked and petted. "Serious fantasies about them..."

Catherine ached and throbbed, her nipples painfully hard. Moisture and longing pooled between her thighs. Luke had to be able to smell how hot he was making her.

Again she struggled to remove the darn dress binding her. But after a few seconds, what Luke was doing took over her every thought. She lay back against the pillows, fisted her hands in her hair and just felt.

"And Lord, your legs," he said hoarsely, skimming both large hands up her thighs. Her muscles bunched and jumped under his expert caress. "I could go on for years about these gorgeous legs. Holy hell, woman. I had more wet dreams about these legs than a man has breakfasts. You laugh. I was a big man about town, and I was salivating over this exquisitely shaped pair."

How could he talk? How could she think? Catherine licked dry lips. "I'm c-covered in freckles."

"Thank you, God." Luke shifted up the bed alongside her. She felt the glide of his hair-roughened thigh travel slowly up hers. "I'm going to spend a long, long time joining the dots. Be patient with me. It'll probably take a lifetime."

Lifetime...?

"I remember the night you stopped being tolerant of me," Catherine murmured. "The girls took me to a strip club. My first time seeing naked guys. My first taste of beer. I came stumbling home and you were standing in the dark kitchen. You wore jeans and a black T-shirt. When I saw you, my heart about jumped out of my chest. I wanted so badly to be sophisticated. Of course, I also wanted to be a petite blonde," she added dryly, wriggling as Luke's agile tongue traveled across her hip.

"You had stars in your eyes and wore a pale yellow dress. It floated around your legs as you dashed across the kitchen and into my arms." His hand skimmed up her thigh, making her breath shudder in her throat.

"You picked me up off my feet and swung me around. It made me dizzy. Then you pressed me against the fridge and kissed me."

"I remember."

"My legs turned to jelly and my head spun. My heart started pounding and my skin went hot, then cold. I'd never felt anything like it."

"You upchucked on my new shoes."

"You pushed me away."

"No. I felt guilty as hell at taking advantage of an innocent young woman who was smashed. I didn't want to compound it by taking you on the kitchen floor."

"One minute you were kissing me like something out of one of my fantasies, the next you were yelling and screaming, absolutely furious that I was drunk and behaving like my mother. You said some really awful things. Made worse by the fact that most of it was true. I *was* a pest. I *was* always underfoot."

"I wanted you so badly I was almost willing to risk Dad killing me. But I thought my touch had revolted you. You were so sick, and you looked at me as though I'd killed your best friend. I wanted that look of sisterly adoration back. But I didn't want you to be my sister."

"I didn't want you to be my brother. I was sick because I'd had too much excitement on top of too much to drink.... Are you going to help me get this stupid dress off my face so I can see you while we have this rather important conversation?"

"In a while. Now, where was I? Ahhh, your belly button." His mouth moved across her middle, then his tongue darted out and licked a sensuous path from navel to hip and back again. Goose bumps rose on her skin and her muscles fluttered. Her hips jerked.

"June 25, your eighteenth birthday party. Fluorescent pink bikini. There were a million nubile young things at that pool party. Nick came with me. I couldn't take my eyes off you. You were practically naked—"

She'd waited with breathless anticipation for Luke to show. He'd arrived late, stayed half an hour. "You left early."

"Pretty hard to hide an erection wearing a swimsuit." He moved up her body, skimming along her sensitized skin and making her shiver and twitch restlessly.

It was with breathless relief that she felt him shift the shroud of fabric covering her head and arms. He found her hand and spread her fingers over his palm. "Now about your hands. Slender, artistic fingers. I love that you never wear polish on your fingernails. I love the way you tap them on the table when you're pissed off. I love when you run your fingers through my hair. Impossible right now, I know. But later..."

He could have at least uncovered her face. Catherine wanted him to kiss her. She wanted to kiss him back. "Are we done with seventeen?"

He flipped the dress back over her tingling hands. "For now. Ah, these shoulders." He stroked what he could reach. "Poets write sonnets about shoulders like these."

"They do support my neck...."

He ignored her. "Slender, yet strong. You carry the weight of the world on these shoulders. You don't need to." He touched two fingers to the base of her throat. "Do you want me, Cat?"

More than my next breath. "What would I do with you if I had you?" she asked lightly, her heart pounding harder, rougher.

"Let me count the ways."

He cupped her left breast in his palm and flicked his thumb over the engorged nipple. The sweet, sharp sensation shot like a flaming arrow to her groin. She moaned. Luke chuckled, but he sounded choked. Catherine felt giddy with desire. High on love. Delirious with hope.

"But first..." his breath whispered across her right breast; his hair tickled her chin "...I need to pay homage to the most incredible pair of breasts it's been my good fortune to meet."

"W-way too small."

"Are you mad, woman? More than a handful is a waste." He proved it. For several minutes the only sound in the room was Luke's mouth against her breasts. The noises alone should be bottled and sold around the world as an aphrodisiac.

His head shifted lower. And lower. Licking, caressing. Touching. Stroking. Until she couldn't tell where Luke ended and she began. He slid down her body until his clever mouth touched her intimately.

"Ah, Cat. The ultimate prize." His tongue opened her slick folds, delving inside. He nuzzled and licked her like an ice-cream cone. She melted when his breath stroked her thighs as he shifted between her legs.

"This—" he licked slowly up her furrow "—was—" down again "—my ultimate fantasy." His tongue darted inside.

Catherine arched off the bed. He held her cold bottom in his hot hands and kissed her again. Hard. Soft. Deep. Shallow.

Catherine forgot to breathe.

"Don't come," Luke told her harshly. "Don't—" he licked her to the edge "—come." He breathed warm air intimately into her, and his fingers tightened on her behind.

Oh, like she could help it? Her body tensed as tight as a bowstring. Every nerve ending quivered for his touch. She was hot enough to melt, so aroused that the next touch would send her over the edge.

Luke shifted across her body. "I'm here. Wait. For. Me." His penis nudged her opening. A sob burst from her lungs as he slid home to the hilt, smooth, hard, impossibly deep. The pleasure took her breath. Tears ran into her hair. She turned her face against her arm as her heart pounded frantically against her ribs. The tribal beat amplified throughout her body. *I love you. I love you. I love you.*

"Wet and wild. But still tight," he murmured, kissing her throat. "Am I hurting you?"

"N-no." She could barely get the word out. Spread wide by his narrow hips, her thighs quivered as he reached between their bodies and rasped his thumb over her sweet spot, circled, pressed.

"Oh my," she managed to pant, as her skin prickled and scalding heat poured through her. Her body arched. "Please."

"Let go, sweetheart. Let go. I have you."

She fell. And Luke was there to catch her.

Like an approaching storm cloud, filled with heat and energy, she felt her body flex and tighten as the climax thundered closer. And closer. And—

Her body convulsed. Luke held her tightly, controlling his own finale to slowly, skillfully rebuild her desire, until she climbed again. Another impossible peak.

"I lo—Yes, sweetheart— *Yes*—"

They came together in a burst of light.

Finally her spasms eased, and she lay sprawled beneath him, their skin bonded and slick with sweat. Luke's chest heaved against hers as he dragged in great gulps of air. She felt him move inside her, and tightened internal muscles to hold him there.

"Ah, Cat." He sighed with satisfaction and stroked a

still-shaking hand down the damp skin of her throat and over her sensitized breast.

"Are you going to help me get this thing off my head, Van Buren?" Catherine murmured.

"Having your head buried is a perfectly crab thing to do."

"That's a *turtle*, not a crab. Come on, Luke. My arms are killing me." Catherine felt as though she were on a high-wire without a net. Either she quickly acknowledged that Luke's ego as a lover had been sorely compromised by their earlier lovemaking, and he'd done that wonderful seduction to prove he still had it, or she could continue this dream....

She loved him so much it was a physical ache in her chest, yet she felt shaky inside, terrified that this would once again blow up in her face.

He lifted his head and she could feel him looking down at her. "Know what I think, my little crab?"

"I tremble to think, my big turkey." She wanted to stay this way forever. Drowsily she nuzzled her fabric-covered nose against his chest. There'd be time later to unveil and have a reality check. But not now. Not when she had him here like this.

"I think you wouldn't recognize Mr. Right if he bit you on the butt."

She yanked the last few remaining strands of hair knotted around the button and freed her face. "You do, do you?"

His eyes danced with little green lights the second they met hers. "Hell, yeah."

She dragged the dress the rest of the way over her head and tossed it on the floor, then looked him in the eye again. They were only a few inches apart. "Maybe he's so blind you wouldn't recognize my butt if it was—was served to y-*him* on a silver platter!" She finished in a rush.

Luke rubbed his chin. Blast his hide, now he was grinning. "Maybe he would."

"Maybe he hasn't."

He bent his head to kiss her lightly on the mouth. "We're getting nowhere fast, aren't we? Boy, I'm going to deserve a medal when this is all over. Cat, Cat. We're going to have to learn to communicate better than this."

She could still feel dried tears on her cheeks. She tried to read his expression, then blinked at what she saw on his face, in his eyes.

He took her face between his hands. "I love you, Cat."

"Love? What about all those emotional eggs in one basket?"

"You are all my emotional eggs, Catwoman. Every last one. You're love, and hope, and promise." His green eyes darkened. "Do you want what's best for me?"

"You know I do."

"You."

"Me what?"

"*You're* what's best for me, Catherine."

"Catherine?"

"I want you to know how serious I am. You're my heart."

"Obligation. Misguided responsibility. A knight in shining *amore* complex."

"*Amore* is exactly what I feel for you. Let me spend the rest of my life showing you how much I love you." He closed his eyes. This was going to kill him if it didn't work.

"Okay," he admitted raggedly before she could interrupt. "I did make you and Dad that promise that I would be your brother and take care of you forever. I made that promise, Cat, with every intention of keeping it. But I haven't felt remotely brotherly for a long time. I fell in love with you, and now I have to break my word."

She smacked him on the arm. "That was when I was a child, you turkey! Why? Why didn't you tell me?"

"Because I thought you needed family more than you needed a temporary lover. I was waiting for you to grow up and make a rational decision about us. But it wasn't you who had to grow up, Cat. It was me."

"Do you love me, Luke? Really love me? Not a morning-after-gee-thanks-that-was-great-sex kinda love. Not, oh my God, I just boinked Cat and now what am I going to do. But the genuine thing?"

"Yeah." He laughed, a joyful, exuberant sound that traveled through her as hot and pure as sunshine. "Love. As in heart and soul. As in crazy about. As in forever."

"You do, huh?" Cat felt a smile blossom from the depth of her being. "What about Mr. Right biting my butt?"

"He'd be more than happy to."

"Yeah?"

"Oh, yeah."

Thrilled at his grumble of protest, she slipped from

beneath him and rolled over onto her stomach. She pointed to her bottom, where the word *LUKE* was tattooed in inch-high red letters.

Luke stared. "Oh, my God. This must've hurt."

She tilted her head to see him better. "Not as much as you not knowing I existed."

"Aw, Cat." His voice sounded gravely soft. He ran a tender finger along the cursive script. "When did you have this done?"

"For my seventeenth birthday. I've always known my Mr. Right. Luke?"

"Yes, my love?" he managed to reply thickly.

"Bite me!"

14

"WE MISSED your mother's wedding. Do you mind?"
Luke asked. He leaned across the armrest between
their seats and played with a lock of her hair. The back
of his hand kept brushing her breast.

"Nah. We'll catch the next one. When you've seen
one, you've seen them all." Catherine touched him intimately under the in-flight magazine on his lap. "Tit
for tat," she whispered naughtily in his ear. Luke
groaned.

He loves me. Catherine wanted to stand on her seat
and yell it to everyone on the plane. She wanted to do
cartwheels down the aisle. *Lucas Van Buren loves me.*

They'd missed the wedding, the reception and saying goodbye. They'd only managed to drag their exhausted bodies out of bed and off to the airport in time
to catch their flight home.

"What's in that bag?" she demanded of the small
sack he'd raced out of the hotel with this morning. "A
present for me?"

"You bet." His eyes gleamed and she felt him twitch
beneath her hand. He wiggled his eyebrows. "I bought
out the hotel's supply of condoms."

She smiled. "How many did you buy?"

"Thirty-three."

Cat almost choked. "Condoms? Thirty-three *condoms*?"

"Too few?" Luke asked, straight-faced. "Don't take offense, Cat. If they'd had more, I would've bought them."

Laughing, she swatted his arm and shifted in her seat. "Behave yourself. We can't do anything—oh, no, Luke. No. Absolutely not—" He kissed her silent.

The captain lit the seat belt sign and announced their imminent arrival in Las Vegas for a brief layover. In a couple of hours they'd be back in San Francisco.

Home. Was there ever a sweeter sound? Home to their big bed. Home to share that big bed. Together. Home with thirty-three condoms.

The second the seat belt sign went off, Luke rose and stepped into the aisle. He held out his hand. "Come on."

"Huh? We don't have to get off."

"I have to stretch my legs."

"And you need me to hold your hand while you do it?" She smiled. "Stay here. I'll keep you so entertained you won't worry about being cramped."

"Not that I don't want to jump at that invitation, but I really do need to stretch out for a bit. Come on, Catwoman, you heard the flight attendant. We'll be sitting in this tin can for another twenty-five minutes." He tugged her hand until she rose. She gave him a curious look before straightening and stepping into the aisle beside him.

The flight attendant, brunette, curvy and petite, gave Luke a smile and a wink. Catherine prodded Luke's back with her elbow and snorted.

As they passed the cockpit area, the attendant leaned toward Luke. "Your fr—"

Luke laid a finger across the woman's mouth. He said something under his breath. She made an expansive gesture with her arm, as if they couldn't have found the wide-open door on their own.

Catherine gritted her teeth.

"Jealous?" he asked, smiling happily as they emerged into the concourse. "Don't worry, sweetheart. If I ever look at another woman, you can cut off my balls."

"Thank you for the offer," Cat said dryly, her amber eyes bright with laughter. "But it was unnecessary. That's something you can definitely count on."

Luke didn't let go of her hand as he tugged her in his wake.

"Hey, look. Slot machines. Got some quarters?" The *kirching* of falling coins blended with announcements of arrivals and departures. Weird. Ignoring her request, Luke kept walking, tugging her behind him.

"Aren't we supposed to stay by the gate?"

"I want something over there." He glanced around, then pointed down the concourse to a flower-bedecked white gazebo sitting incongruously in front of one of the departure gates.

Catherine smiled. "Flowers?"

"Something like that. Come on."

They approached the gazebo, festooned with every kind of flower imaginable and threaded with colorful ribbons. It didn't look like a shop.... Catherine suddenly spotted a guy standing nearby who looked just like— "Nick! Hey, Luke. Look, it's Nick."

"Hey, gorgeous!" Nick braced himself as Cat flung herself into his arms.

Behind her back, Nick gave Luke a thumbs-up. Luke's heart, which hadn't had a normal beat in forty-eight hours, did a somersault. He met the unholy glee in Nick's eyes over her head. Nick grinned and disengaged.

"Thank God," Luke said coolly. "A murder charge would play havoc with business." His best friend's smile widened. And he still had his arm around Cat's shoulders.

"Having a hard time of it, are you, old son?"

"One might say so." Luke scanned the surrounding rows of chairs and the people seated with their backs to them. "Is your assignment complete, good buddy?"

"With a modification, yeah."

"What are you two up to?" Cat demanded, suspicious as hell. She eyed Nick. "Not that it's not delightful to see you, but what are you doing here?"

"Catherine!"

Before he could answer, Cat was swept into the embrace of Molly Cruz, a friend from Beaverton. Behind her stood Sandra Steward, with her husband, Bill, then a dozen old school friends rose from their chairs to converge on her, all talking and laughing at once. Nick had done good.

For several kaleidoscopic moments Cat hugged and exclaimed with her friends. "This is insane! What on earth—"

"Okay, Cat. That's it, time's up." Luke's heart couldn't take much more of this. "Everyone?" He sounded like a movie director, a nervous movie director, as he instructed everyone where to stand. He'd never been so nervous in his life. Luke snatched the bunch of rather wilted daisies from Nick and thrust them into Cat's hands. People parted like the Red Sea to allow Luke to drag her inside the gazebo.

"Luke, what—"

"I want to be your devil's food cake, Cat. We're getting married. Here. Now. Everything else can be ironed out later."

Cat blinked up at him. "Married?"

"Yeah. Got a problem with that?"

Cat smiled. "No."

"Good. Let's do it. Nick, where's the min—"

"Right here." Nick stepped aside to reveal a miniature Elvis Presley. The top of the man's black bouffant do came to Luke's belt buckle. Dressed in a skintight, white sharkskin suit, replete with rhinestones and stand-up collar, the pint-size minister held a black book in his hands and smiled up at them, showing large square teeth.

Cat eased closer to Luke and gripped his hand tightly.

"Dearly beloved..."

"Till death do us part," Luke whispered to a wide-eyed Cat.

"...gathered here..."

Cat pressed her cheek against his shoulder, eyes alight with love and laughter.

"...I want to live in our house together. I want to have children with you. I want us to grow old together. I want commitment, and stability, and knowing we'll have each other for the next sixty or so years. I want it all, Cat."

"...join Catherine and Lucas in holy matrimony..."

"Look at the cake." Luke jerked his chin to a small table supporting a white-frosted wedding cake. "Devil's food."

How Nick had found someone to make this cake at such short notice, Luke had no idea. He owed his friend big time.

The top of the cake held a small basket filled to the brim with eggs. On one side was a tiny orange crab. On the other, a plump turkey. As the minister continued, Luke met Cat's tear-drenched eyes. Her smile lit up his world.

"...man and wife. You may kiss your bride."

*Three sizzling love stories
by today's hottest writers
can be found in...*

Midnight Fantasies....

Feel the heat!

Available July 2001

MYSTERY LOVER—*Vicki Lewis Thompson*

When an unexpected storm hits, rancher Jonas Garfield
takes cover in a nearby cave...and finds himself seduced
senseless by an enigmatic temptress who refuses to tell him
her name. All he knows is that this sexy woman wants him.
And for Jonas, that's enough—for now....

AFTER HOURS—*Stephanie Bond*

Michael Pierce has always considered costume shop
owner Rebecca Valentine no more than an associate—
until he drops by her shop one night and witnesses the
mousy wallflower's transformation into a seductive siren.
Suddenly he's desperate to know her much better.
But which woman is the real Rebecca?

SHOW AND TELL—*Kimberly Raye*

A naughty lingerie party. A forbidden fantasy. When Texas
bad boy Dallas Jericho finds a slip of paper left over from
the party, he is surprised—and aroused—to discover that he
is good girl Laney Merriweather's wildest fantasy. So what
can he do but show the lady what she's been missing....

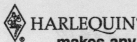

Harlequin invites you to walk down the aisle...

To honor our year long celebration of weddings, we are offering an exciting opportunity for you to own the Harlequin Bride Doll. Handcrafted in fine bisque porcelain, the wedding doll is dressed for her wedding day in a cream satin gown accented by lace trim. She carries an exquisite traditional bridal bouquet and wears a cathedral-length dotted Swiss veil. Embroidered flowers cascade down her lace overskirt to the scalloped hemline; underneath all is a multi-layered crinoline.

Join us in our celebration of weddings by sending away for your own Harlequin Bride Doll. This doll regularly retails for $74.95 U.S./approx. $108.68 CDN. One doll per household. Requests must be received no later than June 30, 2001. Offer good while quantities of gifts last. Please allow 6-8 weeks for delivery. Offer good in the U.S. and Canada only. Become part of this exciting offer!

Simply complete the order form and mail to:
"A Walk Down the Aisle"

IN U.S.A	IN CANADA
P.O. Box 9057	P.O. Box 622
3010 Walden Ave.	Fort Erie, Ontario
Buffalo, NY 14240-9057	L2A 5X3

Enclosed are eight (8) proofs of purchase found on the last page of every specially marked Harlequin series book and $3.75 check or money order (for postage and handling). Please send my Harlequin Bride Doll to:

_____
Name (PLEASE PRINT)

_____
Address   Apt. #

_____
City   State/Prov.   Zip/Postal Code

_____
Account # (if applicable)   098 KIK DAEW

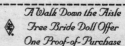

A Walk Down the Aisle
Free Bride Doll Offer
One Proof-of-Purchase

HARLEQUIN®
Makes any time special ®

Visit us at www.eHarlequin.com

PHWDAPOP

If you enjoyed what you just read,
then we've got an offer you can't resist!

Take 2 bestselling
love stories FREE!
Plus get a FREE surprise gift!

Double your pleasure—
with this collection containing two full-length

Harlequin Romance®

novels

New York Times bestselling author

DEBBIE MACOMBER

delivers

RAINY DAY KISSES

While Susannah Simmons struggles up the corporate
ladder, her neighbor Nate Townsend stays home baking
cookies and flying kites. She resents the way he questions
her values—and the way he messes up her five-year plan
when she falls in love with him!

PLUS

THE BRIDE PRICE

a brand-new novel by reader favorite

DAY LECLAIRE

On sale July 2001

HARLEQUIN®

Makes any time special®

Visit us at www.eHarlequin.com

PHROM

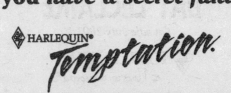